Summer Sin

Northern Witch #4

By K.S. Marsden

K.S. M

Northern Witch

Winter Trials (Northern Witch #1)

Awaken (Northern Witch #2)

The Breaking (Northern Witch #3)

Summer Sin (Northern Witch #4)

Cover by: Lily Dormishev

ISBN: 9798736496921

Chapter One

Mark picked absent-mindedly at the black material of his funeral clothes. His best trousers were stiff and uncomfortable, but some discomfort seemed in keeping with the day.

Only a few hours ago, they had been attending Eadric's funeral, with a dozen witches and friends showing their respect for the pagan ritual.

At the time, Mark had been honoured to be a part of it, and had found solace amongst his coven. But as soon as it was over, he could feel the grief of losing Eadric nipping at his heels. Mark already missed his bright green eyes, and his gentle innocence... gone forever because Mark was foolish enough to drag him into the middle of a witch war.

Mark had tried to keep busy and distract himself, first with his coven; and then visiting Damian in the afternoon, allowing his boyfriend to be his sole focus.

Now though, as Miriam drove him home in silence, stray thoughts plucked at Mark's mind. Eadric's easy smile, and the surprising roughness of his skin when his hand brushed against Mark's.

It was starting to get dark by the time Miriam dropped Mark off, in front of the big farmhouse that was home.

"If you ever need anyone to speak to..." Miriam trailed off. Despite protesting that she was trying to be his friend, she probably knew that teenage-Mark had a slew of friends his own age... "Fine, go, do your thing."

Mark tried to smile his thanks, he knew Miriam was only trying to be nice, but it came off as a bit of an awkward grimace. "I do appreciate it." He said, letting himself out of the car.

The spring evening was mild and calm, and Mark was in no rush to go inside, back to real life. He watched and waved as Miriam's red Audi disappeared down the drive.

When he moved back to the house, movement caught Mark's eye, as a curtain opened in an upstairs window. A pale face hovered, glowering down at him.

"What the-?"

Mark barged through Nanna's empty kitchen, racing up the stairs, two at a time. His initial bravery faded, and he tentatively pushed open the door to the spare room, wary of the monster within.

"Michelle?"

"No, it's sodding Voldemort. Who did you expect?" Came the waspy reply.

Michelle looked her usual angry self, scowling at Mark for daring to exist, never mind his audacity at being in her vicinity.

"Uh, don't take this the wrong way, but why are you here?" Mark asked.

"Why do you think? Your psycho Nanna has kept me trapped in this house since we got back from London!"

"What? Why?"

"She's worried I might go off the rails or cast dark magic." Michelle growled. Holding out her hands, her frown deepened. "I can't... I can't draw on my magic in this prison. She's even blocked reception for my phone – I haven't been able to call for help!"

Mark paused; he knew how that felt. Only a few days ago, he'd had the freakish experience of having his magic out of reach.

"You need to get me out of here." Michelle demanded.

"What... no."

Michelle's eyes widened in disbelief. "Seriously? I risked everything to rescue you from London; you owe me."

"Er... this is nothing alike. You rescued me from a bunch of crazy witches who beat me up and were about to kill me." Mark replied, the bruises were still achingly fresh. "You're stuck with Nanna – who at worst, will overfeed you tea and biscuits."

"I'm still trapped against my will." Michelle snapped, snatching up one of the porcelain figures from the windowsill and throwing it at Mark.

It smashed into the door frame, and Mark backed away from her angry outburst, not wanting to test her throwing skills any further. "OK, OK. I'll see what I can do." He said, holding his hands up defensively.

Mark kept one eye on Michelle, and walked sideways down the stairs. He wouldn't put it past her to push him down the narrow staircase.

"Nanna...?" Under Michelle's scrutiny, his voice wavered. Mark coughed and called again. "Nanna!"

The living room door opened, and Nanna stepped through, still wearing her black funeral clothes.

"What's up, kiddo?" She asked innocently.

"What's up?" Mark echoed. "How about the bloody Wicked Witch of the West trapped in your house?"

Nanna glanced up the stairs, spotting Michelle hovering on the landing. "She's dangerous."

Michelle looked a little smug at the description.

"To us, and herself." Nanna amended. "We can't let a witch juiced up on dark magic loose."

"So, Michelle is going to stay here forever?" Mark asked.

"Not forever." Nanna shrugged. "She's new to dark magic, I'm hoping her addiction won't take long to break."

"You're forgetting, you old bat, I don't want your help." Michelle snapped.

"You say the nicest things." Nanna replied. "Mark, can you please bring Michelle's schoolwork home with you tomorrow. Then you can both train in white magic in the evening."

"What!" Both exclaimed.

Mark was used to having Nanna to himself, and he wasn't sure how he felt sharing her with this angry girl who was pissed off at the world.

"This is pointless, just let me go you crazy witch." Michelle barrelled down the stairs, her murderous glare fixed on Nanna.

"Nanna, watch... out..." Mark's warning faded.

Nanna threw up a hand with a careless gesture and Michelle stopped, stuck behind an invisible barrier. The girl's mouth was opened in scream and slammed her fists against the magical blockade, all noise blocked.

"Thanks for the warning, Mark." Nanna said drily. "I don't know what I would have done if you weren't here."

Mark grunted in response to her sarcasm. "Is this the part where you brag what a powerful witch you are?"

"Well, you do seem to need reminding frequently." Nanna remarked, then nodded in Michelle's direction, where the young girl was still flailing wildly. "She's been having these outbursts all weekend; they fade after a few minutes. We'll be back to sullen teenage silence in no time."

"Holding someone against their will is illegal." Mark pointed out.

"They weren't thinking of magical rehab when they made those rules. Besides, I spoke to Michelle's *legal guardians*." Nanna rolled her eyes. "Her parents didn't even notice she was missing."

On the other side of the invisible barrier, Michelle's tantrum began to fade, just as Nanna predicted. The girl looked exhausted; her rage dissipated into nothing.

"It's late, you should get home before your parents ground you again."

Chapter Two

The next day at school, Mark felt like he was the centre of attention, yet again. It seemed to be the new norm: in the winter term, everyone thought he had used dark magic to attack his classmates; and last term they all thought he'd been cheating on his boyfriend – who was coincidentally their new star striker.

Mark winced as he caught sight of his reflection in one of the windows. He was a bruised and battered mess. The lump on his head was going down, but there was no way to hide the graze across his jaw, and the wicked purple bruise on his face.

Mark wondered what story his classmates would make up this time; it was sure to be good. At least this time, Mark had his supporters back in place.

His best friends, Harry and Sarah, walked ahead. They were being extra-loud, to prove how extra-normal this was. And his boyfriend Damian stood at Mark's side, his fingers nervously brushing his hand.

They had held hands on dates before, and Mark wondered if Damian would dare to do the same at school, especially now they were on a new level. Mark blushed again, as he relived last night, when he'd admitted he was in love with Damian.

Damian hadn't said it back yet, but everything suddenly seemed more serious.

Mark headed to his morning tutor group, and a piece of paper was thrust into his hand.

"Exam timetable?" He read, his heart dropping.

"Yes, we went over it at length, yesterday." His form tutor replied. "I don't know if you remember, but you have your final GCSE exams next month."

Mark rolled his eyes. He couldn't forget if he tried. All his teachers had drilled them over their exams, as though it was news. Mark had lost the will for any original response. "Yes sir." He managed.

"If you have any questions, you know where to find me."

"Yes sir." Mark repeated.

Knowing that he didn't have the teen's attention, his tutor waved a hand to dismiss him.

Mark wasn't allowed to forget about his exams for a second as, when his tutor session drew to a close, every single class and teacher hammered it home. They droned on about the final countdown, and structuring revision, and taking responsibility for yourself.

Mark's head was thumping. He was relieved to make it to dinnertime, and a whole hour's break. He'd no sooner set his tray down at his usual table, than he overheard his fellow students debating the best approach to revision. Mark groaned and dropped his head on the table.

"You alright?"

Mark looked up to see his boyfriend sliding into the chair next to him. "Have you heard: the exams are coming."

Damian bit back a smile. "It might've been mentioned."

"If anyone mentions exams in the next hour, I will stab them with my fork." Sarah warned, waving her blunt weapon.

"Noted." Mark grinned at the threat posed by the petite blonde girl.

"In more important news, *before* we got kidnapped by dark witches and threatened with death and torture..." Sarah announced with a dismissive wave of her hand. "Harry totally rocked on stage, and his fan-base is growing!"

"That's awesome." Mark replied, his voice not quite sounding right. He was thrilled that Harry's fledgling singing career was taking off, but he couldn't forget that the dark witches and their death threats his friends had suffered were all his fault.

Edith and her coven had only kidnapped Harry and Sarah to lure Mark out of hiding. Mark had a long way to go before he made it up to his friends. It was already too late to make it up to Eadric...

Mark felt pressure on his arm, and he saw Damian leaning against him, a look of concern crossing his face.

"I'm fine." Mark insisted.

Harry didn't seem to notice the exchange; he was too busy listing the venues that his 'manager' was negotiating with. "The Warehouse in Leeds have already asked me to come back, and there's loads'a places in Sheffield I want to perform."

Mark forced a weak smile; he could well believe that Harry wanted to do a gig in the hometown of his favourite band. Hell, Harry probably already saw himself warming up for the Artic Monkeys.

"Anywhere but London..." Harry pulled a face. "We've learnt our lesson – no more venues owned by demons, or in league with evil witches. My manager is going to do thorough background checks from now on."

"Sounds like a lotta work."

Sarah smiled adoringly at her boyfriend. "He's worth it."

"Wow, I've never seen the mushy thing up close." Damian hissed in Mark's ear. "You're right, they're very intense."

Mark snorted a laugh, receiving weird looks from his friends. "Y'know, you still owe Dean a gig."

"What?"

"He was at the gig in Leeds – he promised not to tell the other students, if you'd perform at his next party." Mark saw their confusion change to concern. "Sorry, I thought I'd told you."

"Nah, you were too busy making eyes at Eadric." Harry broke off when he received a less-than-subtle punch from Sarah. "Oh, is that the time? We have to, um..."

Harry stood up, his empty plate rattling on the table. Sarah escorted him briskly out of the food hall, before he could embarrass them any further.

"Well, that was uncomfortable." Mark remarked, his humour not hitting the right note.

"Look, I don't judge you for anything that happened after I broke up with you." Damian said. He sounded sincere, but he didn't raise his eyes from the table.

"*Nothing* happened..." Mark stressed. Maybe if he said it often enough, he'd believe it too.

*****

Mark headed home, with his rucksack digging into his shoulder, as he tried to fit two bulky folders in it. Both folders contained a breakdown of the exams. Mark wondered how long it would be before Michelle threw her copy out of the window. He didn't know why Nanna insisted that he brought Michelle's work home, there wasn't a chance in hell that she'd do anything more productive than turn it into confetti.

Mark made his way into Nanna's kitchen, the kettle already boiling on the Aga, and a plate of biscuits on the table.

Michelle came stomping down the stairs as Mark poured the tea. Her brow raised disdainfully. "This is too cute." She muttered, pinching a biscuit.

"You don't have to be here."

Michelle snorted. "Have you forgotten that I'm trapped in this house? What am I supposed to do, stay in my bedroom until your Nanna magically decides to release me?"

It wasn't *her* bedroom, Mark wanted to argue, a new and surprising territorial feeling over his family's house.

"It's fine." Mark replied curtly. "I brought your homework."

Michelle ignored the folder that was dumped on the table, her dark-brown eyes were fixed on Mark with an unsettling gaze.

"That passive-aggressive thing don't work." She stated. "You keep sayin' you're fine, but you never mean it – I can see your anger, and so can everyone else."

"I'm not angry-"

"Fine; frustrated, upset, in pain..." Michelle interjected. "Your fella died. Why even pretend you're OK?"

The dark energy that had been bubbling inside Mark all day surged up again. His coven had paid tribute to Eadric at yesterday's pagan funeral, which had provided a temporary boon.

Now that he acknowledged its existence, the darkness threatened to rush back. The pain, the grief, and the guilt that Eadric had given his life to save Mark.

"My coven helped start the healing." He argued.

Michelle snorted inelegantly. "Save all that touchy-feely crap. What you really need is to scream."

"What?" Mark blurted out.

"Don't look at me gone out." Michelle protested. "It ain't illegal. Dare you to scream."

A strangled noise came out of Mark's throat, before he coughed and blushed. "I don't think-"

Michelle interrupted him with an ear-splitting scream.

Once Mark got over his shock, he felt the pressure rise to join in. He started to scream, pathetic at first, his voice wobbling, before he put some oomph behind it.

Michelle caught his eye and they both broke into laughter.

The dark part that had been stirring now settled back down, sated for now.

"You were right, it worked." Mark confessed.

Michelle nodded; her smile being replaced by her usual sneer. "Still not your friend." She pointed out.

"What the blazes?"

Mark turned to see Nanna standing in the doorway, looking at them in disbelief.

"I thought someone was bein' murdered."

Mark gulped. "Um, no, Michelle was sharing some stress-relief theories."

Nanna shook her head. "Why can't you just scrap, like normal kids?"

Mark hid his smile behind his cup of tea.

"Right, we're gonna do some basic crystal work today. The moon is still full enough to be useful." Nanna announced. "I've only got one book, so you'll have to share for your homework."

"Share?" Michelle spat. "I'm not doing some namby-pamby white magic."

Nanna crossed her arms. "You are if you ever want to do magic again. We don't allow dark magic around here."

"You don't control me."

"Of course I don't, dearie." Nanna replied drily. "I'll just keep you trapped in here, blocked from dark magic, until you change your mind. If it takes months, years... I'm in no rush."

Michelle's usually-pasty complexion whitened further at the threat.

Nanna grabbed a wide wooden box and placed it on the kitchen table. When she opened it, she revealed stones and gems of various colours and shapes.

"Crystals can help bring balance, and provide energy to boost the strength of your spells." Nanna reeled off, gesturing to the box. "Select a crystal, and we'll practise pouring energy into them, for later use."

"This is why dark magic is better. It's strong on its own." Michelle scowled at the box. "These aren't all *crystals* anyway."

"It's a generic term girly." Nanna replied. "And the sooner you pull that stick out of your arse and give it a go, the sooner your lesson will be over."

Mark bit his tongue, there was something satisfying about Nanna taking on the school bully.

He turned to the task, remembering what Nanna had previously told him about the importance of picking your own stone. He felt a pull towards an unpolished garnet with a dark, purplish hue.

Mark watched as Michelle's hand snapped out and picked up a lump of jet.

"Jet is protective by nature, it's a good stone to have." Nanna commented. "Now, call the quarters to create a neutral workspace. Michelle, if you struggle to envision them, you can use elements to back you up."

When Nanna's back was turned, Michelle raised her hand in a rude gesture.

"Y'know the glass cabinet is reflective." Nanna remarked. "Mark, you can help Michelle find her zen."

Both Mark and Michelle groaned loudly.

Nanna made herself comfortable, in the corner of the kitchen, opening her latest copy of Cosmo.

Calling the quarters was becoming easy for Mark, and as he slipped into the zone, a familiar calm greeted him. His attention was forced back to reality, as he saw Michelle glowering at him.

"Y'know, the growly witch routine is getting old." He remarked. "Do you want help?"

"No." Michelle snapped.

"Uh huh, sure." Mark got up from his seat and rummaged around the kitchen, pulling out utensils to represent the elements. A bowl of water for West; a pot of earth and basil to the North; an empty bowl of air to the East. Finally, with a little focus, Mark set a candle alight for the South point.

Michelle watched him with extreme wariness and derision at his reliance on natural magic; but when all the four points were honoured, her eyes fluttered shut. Michelle's breath stilled, and a look of pure peace crossed her face. Without her trademark anger and rage, she looked like a stranger.

Mark could sense the little jet stone drawing out her darkness like a poison.

Michelle jolted away, looking accusingly at Mark. Panic fuelled her brown eyes.

Michelle pushed her chair back, the legs screeching across the tile floor. She fled upstairs without a word, leaving Mark sitting alone in stunned silence.

Nanna put down her magazine, gazing curiously at the aftermath.

"What...?"

"Jet protects against darkness; it also helps balance and heal the soul." Nanna gave a bitter smile. "Poor Michelle, being at peace is a completely foreign concept to her. No wonder she freaked out."

Mark stared at the empty chair next to him. He didn't understand Michelle, she actively chose the darkest path. The school bully, the dark witch, the demon's mistress. She only had herself to blame.

"She could do with a friend right now." Nanna prompted.

Knowing how futile it was to argue, Mark snatched up the abandoned black stone and stomped upstairs. He knocked on the spare bedroom door.

"Sod off."

Mark braced himself for further thrown knick-knacks, as he opened the door. This time, Michelle was sat quietly on the single bed, with a very familiar ginger cat in her lap.

"Traitor!" Mark gasped.

"What?" Michelle was so surprised, a hurt expression slipped past her mask.

"No, not you." Mark said, gesturing to the cat. "Tigger."

"Is that his name?" Michelle scratched him under the chin. "He's been keeping me company for the last couple of days. At least he doesn't judge me, do you, pretty boy?"

Mark watched the bizarre scene of the big-bad-bully cooing to the fluffy cat. Tigger purred, enjoying the attention thoroughly.

"We're only trying to help." Mark said gently.

"Well, be less helpful."

Mark leant against the doorframe. "How did you get tangled up in demons and dark magic?"

"Robert found me. He opened my eyes to the real world. After years of feeling like I was living a false life, he offered me the truth, and to connect with my real family." Michelle shrugged. "For a price."

"Yeah, he likes his bargains." Mark muttered. "What did you have to do, use dark magic for him?"

"Hell no, that was my prize. You can be as judgy as you like, but dark magic was power, in a world where I'd always been powerless. I didn't care where it came from." Michelle rolled her eyes. "No, Robert wanted my help. It started with little stuff, bringing him up-to-date after his stint in demon prison. Teaching him to use a phone, y'know."

"And then?"

Michelle hugged Tigger closer to her chest, staring resolutely at the wall.

"Was it worth it?"

Michelle gave a weird tilt of her head. "He followed through on his side of the bargain. Trained me up in dark magic, and delivered me to my mother."

"But-?" Mark frowned, not following the logic. As far as he recalled, her parents lived in Tealford. Mark had seen her mother working at the local bank, and knew she had nothing to do with witchcraft.

"I'm adopted." Michelle mumbled.

"I had no idea!"

"Well, it's not bleedin' public knowledge." Michelle snapped with a reassuring bite. "I've always known. Dunno why my parents took me in, they don't give two shits about me. I tried to find info on my birth parents, but no luck. Then Robert turned up with stories about my birth-mother."

"Oh... um, cool?" Mark said weakly, not knowing what the standard response was supposed to be. "So... was your mum part of Edith's coven?"

Michelle gave him a dead stare, waiting for him to catch up.

The penny finally dropped.

"Edith?"

Michelle gave a slow nod, focussing on the warm cat again.

"Woah." No wonder Mark had thought that Edith looked familiar. In fact, with her dark brown hair and slightly-cruel aura, he wondered how he'd missed it. "Who else knows?"

"No one. I don't really want to advertise that I'm the spawn of the witch that nearly killed everyone." Michelle scowled at him. "If you tell anyone, I'll kill you."

"Noted." Mark rolled the lump of jet in his palm. "Here, you forgot this."

He placed it on her dresser, the black stone looking small and innocent.

"I know that using natural magic isn't as flashy as your demon-fuelled stuff, but I think you should give it a go." Mark shrugged. "Besides, it'd be nice not to be the only witch-in-training here."

Chapter Three

After school the next day, Mark got off the bus early, and made his way to Denise's house.

The last time he'd been here was following Eadric's funeral. The pain of his passing was still fresh, and Mark's grief was at odds with the bright and beautiful spring day.

He hesitated, before knocking firmly on the door. A few minutes later, Denise answered, her hair a freshly-dyed bright purple, and her usually-brilliant smile somewhat dimmed.

"Hello dearie, blimey you look a mess. Are you putting arnica on those bruises?" Denise remarked, peering closer at his black eye. "Sorry lad, what brings you here?"

"I wanted to check how you were doing. Sorry, I should've brought food or... something. That's the social norm, isn't it?" As Mark rambled on, he ran a nervous hand through his hair. "Sorry, I forgot what I was saying."

Denise smiled knowingly. "Come on in, I just put the kettle on."

Mark followed the older woman through her house, and in no time was sitting at her kitchen table, nursing a mug of herbal tea. Mark nearly choked as he gazed at the empty seat beside him.

"Eadric made such an impact on us all, in the short time he was with us." Denise said, unusually gentle. "I miss him too."

"I can't believe he's gone. It's all my fault." Mark sighed; his hands wrapped firmly around the warm, comforting mug. "I should've tried harder to keep him away from London."

Denise snorted. "You underestimate how stubborn that boy was."

"Then I shouldn't have brought him here in the first place." Mark argued.

"I've no idea what freaky magic you used to pull him out of his timeline, but from what Silvaticus has told us, you saved him from a fate worse than death. He's at peace now."

Mark twisted the mug in his hands. Eadric had admitted he feared being trapped with Silvaticus in eternal torment – the perfect punishment from their enemy Robert. "Do you believe that?"

Denise gave him a gentle squeeze on the shoulder. "Death is a complete mystery. You're young and this is the first time you've lost anyone. I'm much more educated on the subject, I'd like to believe he's at peace."

Mark sat quietly, Denise's words were well-meaning, but not completely effective at alleviating his guilt and grief. "How's Danny getting on with Silvaticus?"

Denise shrugged, "Well, everyone is still in one piece and the demon hasn't used him to take over the world, so I'd say the gamble paid off. He's in the garage, if you want to see him."

"Really?"

"Yeah, he's been stopping by after work every day to check in, and prove he's still in control. We want to trust Silvaticus, but he's still a demon."

*****

Mark headed over to the garage at the edge of Denise's crazy and colourful gardens. As he walked over the gravel, he could hear a rhythmic thudding, that got louder as he approached the old red-brick garage.

Mark let himself in, to find the interior had been turned into an amateur gym. Mis-matched weights were stacked at one side, and some shiny new gym mats were propped up against the opposite wall.

In the centre, was a battered punching bag, being hit by a sweaty-looking Danny. The History teacher's arms were skinny and unimpressive, and his boxing technique was shoddy, but he was throwing a surprising amount of force behind each blow.

Danny eventually noticed Mark hovering in the doorway and broke off from his work-out.

"Hey."

"Hey." Danny grabbed a towel and wiped away the moisture that glistened on his face and neck.

Mark chewed on his lip. He'd never really gotten on with Danny, but he still felt somewhat responsible for the position he was now in. "You OK?"

"Yeah, I've just got a lot of excess energy right now." He nodded to the various apparatus. "I had to knock the dust off this stuff."

"You look pretty strong."

Danny shrugged. "Silvaticus says it's a side-effect of our union. Because I'm a willing host, I get some of his strength."

"What's it like having him with you?" Mark asked. Damian's experience had been one of darkness and blackouts; Mark couldn't imagine Silvaticus would be as cruel.

"It's... weird. I feel like a stranger in my own skin. What with the extra strength, and my magic doesn't feel as stable as before. I can sense him, he's like an extension of me that I never knew existed. He's still tired from the battle at Ostara, and I can feel his grief over Eadric trickle through. His emotions are intense and make mine pale in comparison. I've never felt affection for anyone, like

Silvaticus has for his former hosts." Danny's voice dropped, and he broke off.

The silence grew longer and more awkward. Mark could sense Danny's uncertainty, which seemed at complete odds with the History professor's usual confidence.

Mark realised that even know-it-all adults didn't *actually* know everything.

"You're coping, though?" Mark asked, with a frown. "I know we're not close, but if your ever need someone to talk to..."

Danny snorted at Mark's comment, with a reassuringly-familiar disdain. He tried to turn it into a cough, and gave a forced smile. "Thanks."

*****

Mark stepped into Nanna's empty kitchen, a little disappointed that nobody was there. He noticed the stairs were littered with broken paraphernalia.

Not wanting to tackle the assault course, Mark checked the living room for life first.

"Nanna?"

Nanna was sitting in her favourite armchair, nursing a cup of tea, the tv blaring in front of her. Tigger curled in her lap, as a bright orange ball of fur.

"You're watching Umbrella Academy?" Mark asked, smirking as he recognised the scene.

"Michelle insisted that, if I was going to continue keeping her captive, I had to at least join the Netflix revolution." Nanna shrugged. "Some of these shows aren't bad, and they've got the full collection of Fifty Shades."

Mark's laugh was cut short by a growing rumble upstairs, followed by a deafening crash.

Nanna sighed. "It's a bad day today."

There was another smash that resonated through the house.

"If she's so averse to our help, why don't we just let her go?" Mark finally asked what had been eating away at him. "All we seem to be doing is causing her pain."

"A little pain now will stop a lot of hurt later on, trust me." Nanna paused as a muffled scream echoed above them. "We just need patience, she may be lashing out at the world, but there's just a scared little girl beneath it all."

Mark bit his tongue. It was hard to imagine anything scared or little underneath all of Michelle's venom and bluster.

"Is there anything I can do to help?"

Another crash sounded upstairs. Nanna sighed and looked to the ceiling. "Be patient. And be there for her, she'll need a friend."

Mark snorted. "Michelle has made it clear that we will *never* be friends."

"What she wants, and what she needs are two very different things." Nanna remarked. "Maybe you could show her she's not alone. She'll be able to relate to you more than my old bones."

Mark watched as his all-powerful Nanna idly stroked the pampered house cat, and an idea began to brew. Now he just had to face the roaring dragon above.

"Wish me luck." He muttered.

Before he could change his mind, Mark headed back to the kitchen, stopping to sweep up some supplies, before he made his way upstairs.

Mark dodged the debris as best he could, fragments of glass and pottery crushing to dust under his trainers. He knocked sharply on the spare bedroom door.

"Go away." Michelle shouted.

Mark slowly pushed it open, wary of any more flying missiles. Luckily, it seemed that Michelle was out of ammunition. "Hey."

"Are you freakin' deaf?" Michelle demanded; her voice hoarse from screaming. Her hair was a wild mess, and her eyes red from crying, her face ghostly pale.

Mark rubbed his thumb over the bag of supplies. "I thought you might want... a distraction; some company maybe."

"I thought the 'go away' was pretty self-explanatory. I don't want you or anybody else." Michelle snarled.

"I wasn't thinking of my company..." Mark called on Luka. The black and white collie appeared at his side, calmly nudging Mark's hand.

Mark heard Michelle take a sharp breath in. Her bloodshot eyes were fixed on the dog.

"He's not going to hurt you." Mark said gently, rubbing Luka's ears.

"I have this thing about dogs, ever since I got bit as a child." Michelle said through gritted teeth.

"Oh, I'm sorry, I didn't realise." Mark said with a pang of guilt. He looked down at Luka, who wagged his tail happily. "Technically, he's not a dog. He's a protective spirit that just chooses this form... I don't know why."

"It don't matter." Michelle waved in Luka's direction. "He's still dog-shaped."

She was looking so agitated; Mark's guilt began to swell, that he was providing the cause of her stress. "I can... show you how to call your own protective spirit."

"Really?" Michelle asked, an unusual spike of interest in her voice.

"Yeah, I'm sure it's only a matter of time before Nanna taught you." Mark said with a shrug.

Mark looked over at Michelle, wondering what creature would manifest as her protective spirit. He allowed Luka to dissipate into thin air, then turned his attention to the spell.

"You need to get some monkshood, sticklewort, fennel, and mugwort." Mark directed, as he rolled out the herbs and a small hessian bag. Mark grabbed the spell book, flicking to the right page.

Michelle slowly browsed Nanna's herb inventory, not having been brought up with it, like Mark. She hesitated as she pulled out the four dried samples.

"You need to put them in the pouch and add a drop of blood."

Michelle did so, hardly flinching as she used a sharp knife to draw blood from her fingertip.

Mark passed her the spell to recite. "This will call a spirit who will protect you when you feel fear. With practise, you can call them at will. Nanna told me that the weaker the witch, the stronger the spirit."

"I'm surprised you don't have a dragon, then." Michelle said bitterly.

Mark rolled his eyes, no longer impressed by her snide comments. She was no longer the scary school bully, and her remarks were starting to lose their effect.

Realising she wasn't getting a rise out of him, Michelle huffed and turned back to the spell book. She started to recite, her voice hoarse and croaking, but determined to finish.

"Pure of heart, kind of soul;

"I seek the protective spirit.

"Hear my fears, mark them well;

"Bring one that will stop harm."

There was a waft of warm air, and a creaking sound. Mark turned to see a large black bird perching on the chair.

"Is that... a crow?" Michelle asked, an honest smile breaking out.

"Yeah, looks like." Mark said, as the bird ruffled its feathers.

Michelle reached out, gently running her fingers over the animal, her grin widening as she realised that it was physically there. "OK, for natural magic, this is pretty cool."

Chapter Four

Mark was quickly falling into a routine. School, followed by training in Nanna's kitchen with Michelle. Afterwards, Mark would leave the imprisoned girl behind, and spend the evening with his friends and boyfriend.

Boyfriend: the term still sent chills, and made Mark grin like a mad fool.

"By the Dark Lord, if I ever look as goofy as you, please put me out of my misery." Michelle interjected when Mark got lost in his thoughts.

"Gladly." Mark retorted. "And using the word 'please'; you are making progress."

Michelle snorted and lobbed a biscuit at his head.

Mark was about to retaliate, when Nanna walked through the back door.

"You two are worse than bloody toddlers. I can't leave you alone for a minute." She moaned, as she kicked off her muckers.

"I'll grow up when you do." Mark grinned. "Nanna... are you wearing make-up?"

Nanna chewed a lip that was unnaturally lustrous. "And what if I am? As a grown woman, I'm entitled to do what I like, irrespective of the feelings of any grandchildren or wards."

Mark leant closer. "You've got mascara on and everything! I thought that you said you didn't wear make-up 'cos you were so naturally beautiful, it was unfair to have a further advantage!"

Across the table, Michelle raised a brow, obviously not used to Nanna's lack of humility.

"I decided to make an exception today." Nanna crossed her arms defensively.

Mark looked from his dolled-up Nanna to the scuffed horsey boots she'd just kicked off. A suspicion slowly rose. "Did you have the new farrier today? The one everyone's raving about?"

"Perhaps." Nanna replied airily.

"And the verdict is?" Mark prompted.

"Ugh, that man is sinfully good-looking. He should come with a health warning." Nanna sighed, dropping into her chair. "Derek's in his fifties, and has the arse and arms of a god."

"Derek?" Michelle piped up. "It's not exactly a sexy name."

"You can judge for yourself, when you meet him." Nanna fanned herself with her magazine. "I'm seeing him for drinks at the weekend, then I thought I'd invite him to Beltane."

"I thought he wasn't sticking around long?" Mark asked.

"He's not, just a few weeks."

"So, it's just a quick fling." Michelle sniped.

"Ugh, I wouldn't mind being flung by him..."

"Nanna!" Mark and Michelle shouted in unison, before bursting into laughter.

"You kids are so bloody sensitive. Fine..." Nanna grabbed a thick book, and dropped it on the table. The single word 'Herbs' was embossed on the cover.

"Right, you two are gonna read about the proper care and storage of herbs, and the benefits of dried versus fresh." Nanna said, with a mischievous glint in her eye.

Mark groaned at the ridiculously dull work. "I thought we were proving to Michelle how *cool* natural magic is?"

"That was before you took the mick out of me and Derek." Nanna replied airily. She tucked her magazine under her arm and headed to the living room. "Give me a shout if you need any help."

"Your Nanna's..." Michelle broke off.

"Immature?" Mark offered. "Insane? Impossible?"

"Interesting." Michelle finished.

"She can also hear through doors." Nanna's voice piped up from the next room. "I'll take 'interesting' as a compliment. It's much nicer than what you normally call me, girly."

Mark smiled and turned his attention to the thick tome that sat between them. Knowing Nanna wasn't going to change her mind any time soon, he opened the book, trying not to groan at the dense pages of text.

Mark and Michelle sat in silence, the subject matter was incredibly dry and neither of them were motivated to discuss it any further. As they went on, Mark found his reading getting slower, as he had to go over the same paragraph several times to attempt to absorb it. After this punishment, he was never going to take the piss out of Nanna and the farrier again. Well, at least not for a week.

A rap at the door broke Mark's concentration from the latest herb entry. Not hiding his relief, he got up, and was even more pleased to see Damian hovering outside.

Mark had no sooner opened the door, than he realised his mistake. The person might look like Damian, but the confident swagger and the black eyes were a giveaway.

"Robert. It's been what, two weeks? Isn't that a record for not causing chaos?"

"Mark." The demon's eyes narrowed. "If that was an attempt at humour, it was very poor."

"Why are you here?" Mark demanded, cutting to the point.

A knowing smile curled at Robert's lips, making Mark shiver.

"Business. Which is alas quite pressing, otherwise..." Robert climbed onto the first step, bringing him that much closer to Mark. "I would love to spend a few hours with you-"

Whatever Robert was going to say was interrupted by a heavy textbook being thrown at his head. The demon's look of surprise was priceless, but he quickly turned back to smug when he spotted his assailant.

"Why Michelle, my little minion. This is where you've been hiding." Robert leant back, to look at the house anew, reading the spells that were blocking his magic. "Impressive."

"Leave this house." Michelle hissed.

Mark could see the girl was trembling, so close to the source of her dark magic.

"*Leave me.*" She demanded.

A knowing smile curled the corner of Robert's lips. "My dear, it is only a matter of time before you come back on your knees, *begging*. What a delicious idea."

"Michelle, go upstairs." Nanna's voice came from within the house.

Michelle moved obediently to the stairs, but only made it as far as the first step, hovering like a shadow.

Nanna walked to the door, meeting Robert's gaze unflinchingly.

"Demon." She greeted.

"Witch." Robert returned, his gaze flicking from the shield, to the powerful witch who'd cast it.

"You can't have the girl." Nanna warned. "She's no longer yours."

"Don't get worked up, your Grand Highness. At least not on Michelle's account." Robert smiled at Mark. "Your grandson owes me a favour. I'm here to collect."

Nanna crossed her arms, standing next to Mark, defensively.

"There's nothing you can do. The contract is between me and the boy." Robert pointed out.

Mark squirmed, thinking back on his offer of a favour, in return for Robert's help. He had the feeling that Robert's request would be wild.

"I'm not inviting you in." Nanna growled, her magic pulsing.

His stubborn Nanna versus the deceptive Robert. Mark wondered if the house would still be standing if those two titans clashed. He sighed and stepped outside, leaving his Nanna's protective spell.

"Mark-" Nanna warned.

"It's OK. He won't hurt me." Mark said, sounding calmer than he felt. "He's had plenty of opportunities."

"But Mark-"

"Trust me." He shrugged. "Besides, he's hardly gonna kill me if he expects my help."

Nanna pursed her lips, but didn't argue any further.

Taking her silence as permission, Mark strode away, to the very edge of the garden. Once they were out of earshot of the house, Mark leant against the stone wall, waiting for Robert to get on with his master scheme.

With remarkable ease, the demon leapt up, perching on top of the wall. His intense dark eyes bore into Mark's. Despite his claim that business was urgent, he appeared to be in no great rush.

"What do you want?" Mark urged, crossing his arms.

Robert's eyes brightened and a sly smirk played across his lips.

Mark sighed; he'd forgotten who he was talking to. The horny-demon act was wearing thin. "What do I have to do to repay your favour?"

Robert leant back, narrowing his black eyes. "You really do sap the fun out of everything, Mark. If you want to mix business with pleasure, I'd be delighted to show you a few tricks I've learnt over the centuries."

"I'm not here to be your minion or sex slave." Mark stressed, not wanting to risk thinking about Robert's experience. "I just want to do the bare minimum to cancel out my debt."

"Pity. I bet there are things you've fantasised about doing with Damian. I'd be more than willing to re-enact them; you could even pretend I was him-"

"Robert!" Mark snapped, a red blush creeping up his neck.

"Fine, back to business." Robert sighed. "Those hell beasts are still hunting me, and it's getting fairly tiresome constantly fighting them. I need you to contact who's sending them and negotiate their cessation."

"You want me to do what now?" Mark asked, his jaw dropping at Robert's request. "I'm not getting messed up in any more demon shit. Find someone else."

"No, you'll just summon demons and use the demon road when it is of benefit to you." Robert sneered. "Besides, it's only fitting that you call off the hunt. You freed Silvaticus from the trap for which I was imprisoned. If Silvaticus is no longer trapped in an eternal hell of pain and torture, then I don't see why I should remain guilty for imprisoning him."

Mark groaned. He didn't know if this weird logic was common amongst demons, or just Robert's skewed way of looking at things. "I wouldn't even know where to start."

"You're rather friendly with Silvaticus and his new host. Talk to him."

"*You* talk to him. Especially if you're as innocent as you claim."

Robert leant uncomfortably close to Mark. "I could, but then I'd have to think of... *something else* you can do to pay me back..."

Mark pushed away from the wall, wanting to put a little distance between them. "Fine, I'll see what I can do."

"Oh, such confidence-inspiring promises..."

"Aren't you too old for sarcasm?" Mark didn't wait for an answer, starting to walk back to his family's house. "After this, we're even. You can go possess someone else, and leave us all alone."

"But I'm enjoying this one so very much." Robert crooned. "And he's not entirely unwilling."

"I- what?"

"Haven't you noticed? Damian has been getting stronger, since you persuaded him to work with me at Ostara. We're moving towards that symbiotic relationship that Silvaticus is always blathering about." Robert said, victory in his quiet voice. "Damian suspects the truth. I wonder if he would even give me up, if he had the choice."

Mark felt a chill run down his spine. He hadn't even considered that danger; and thanks to Mark's lack of knowledge, he'd forced Damian into an even worse position. "You're lying."

"I can't lie." Robert reminded him. "You should ask your boy toy next time you see him."

Mark stood numbly for a moment, before heading for the safety of his house.

Chapter Five

Robert's unexpected visit did have one positive result. Nanna decided that Michelle's reaction to the demon was a sign that the initial dark magic addiction had lost its hold on her.

"Tomorrow, you can go back to school." Nanna announced.

Michelle quickly went from looking proud from the open praise she'd received, to looking mortified. "That's not a reward; that's like, the opposite of a reward. I think I've earnt a trip to Disneyland, or at the very least, Flamingo Land."

"Don't worry." Mark piped up. "If you behave for the rest of term, she might take you for an ice-cream."

Michelle scowled and threw a biscuit at him. She was getting so predictable, that Mark managed to catch it, chomping down on the custard cream.

"Mark, you're gonna keep an eye on her at school." Nanna said, ignoring their immature actions.

Michelle groaned loudly. "I don't need a babysitter."

"Yeah, you do." Nanna countered. "You've worked so hard, and come so far. I want to make this transition as easy as possible. Mark, watch her."

Michelle huffed. "He's too *busy* with his friends and boyfriends, and his perfect life."

"Uh, boyfriend – singular. I'm a one-man-guy." Mark pointed out.

"Sure you are." Michelle rolled her eyes. "Damian, Robert, that Eric guy."

"Eadric." Mark corrected out of habit. Technically, their brief whatever-it-was occurred after Damian had broken up with Mark. "And nothing's going on with Robert. At all."

"Sure."

*****

The next morning, Mark headed to the bus stop with Michelle in tow. They walked in an awkward silence – Mark had tried to make small-talk, but Michelle had only bristled and snapped at him.

Despite her protests that she was glad to leave the house, Mark could sense her anxiety, as Michelle's aura pulsed a familiar, ugly brown.

When the school bus rumbled up, Mark took his usual seat. The other students always left that bench open, so Damian could join him when they finally got to his stop. Mark looked up to Michelle, wondering if she would want to sit next to him.

"Um..." He said gormlessly.

Michelle bared her teeth at his inelegant attempt at friendship, and headed to the back row, to join the other trouble-makers.

When they arrived at school, Harry and Sarah also joined them, making Michelle the fifth wheel.

"Michelle, you look... good." Sarah said, in honest surprise, not having seen the girl since her rehab began.

Michelle growled a very sweary reply, making Sarah take a wary step back.

"She's still working on her reaction to positive comments." Mark explained as a sort of apology. "Are you joining us for dinner, Michelle?"

Michelle looked hurt by Mark's open commentary on her character flaws. She pushed past him, elbowing him hard in the ribs. "I'm still not your friend."

*****

The morning passed slowly, each class boringly repetitive, as the teachers condensed all their previous work into exam-focussed study. Mark found his attention quickly waning, and spent a lot of his time observing his fellow students.

After several weeks of Mark and Damian quietly dating, with no further black eyes or magical attacks, the rumour mill had died down. Some of the students still looked at Mark warily, but he no longer felt that the mob was ready to lynch him, or burn him for being a dark witch. He only hoped that Robert stayed away, and things remained quiet for the rest of term.

Mark headed to lunch, for more chips with a side of chips. As he sat at his usual table with Damian, Harry and Sarah, Mark wondered where Michelle had her lunch. He couldn't remember ever seeing her in the dinner hall.

"So, I've been in touch with the organisers at Doncaster's Fake Fest. We're too late to get into this year's gig, but they'll sign us up for next year." Sarah announced.

"Doncaster?" Harry pulled a face at the thought of going to the old mining town.

"What's up with Doncaster?" Damian asked quietly, the poor Southener completely lost in the conversation.

"It doesn't have the same musical heritage as Sheffield, but it's made real strides lately." Sarah argued. "They're supporting a lot of local artists."

"Hey, you might meet Yungblud." Mark grinned. "Or that dude from One Direction."

"We've got a couple of new venues in Bradford and Wakefield interested, too." Sarah said, expertly steering the conversation back to what she considered important. "This is all becoming a reality for Harry – soon we'll have to turn them away!"

"I hate to be a buzz kill, but remember to book his exams into his timetable." Mark said, earning scathing looks from his friends.

Sarah's phone beeped, claiming her attention. "Oh, someone's messaged me on Insta about a gig..."

She scrolled through and frowned at the username. "Dean?"

Everyone twisted in their seats, to spy their fellow-student sitting a couple of metres away.

"You could have just spoke to us, Dean." Sarah pointed out.

"Yes, but you guys can get so *snippy* when I interrupt your very important conversations." Dean shrugged. "Besides, I want to make an official booking in writing. I want Not-Dave to sing at my pre-exam party next Friday."

Harry groaned, "Look, I know that you think I owe you a gig, and probably think this is a lark; but I see performing as my profession. I'm saving for driving lessons – I'll do a song for free, but-"

"I'm gonna pay." Dean broke in, frowning at Harry's misunderstanding. "I'm not asking for a freebie, or 'mates' rates'. Besides, you guys are always clear that we're not mates."

Having said his piece, Dean picked up his tray and made a hasty exit from the dining hall.

The table fell into an awkward silence. Dean was annoying, and they might not *like* him, but they didn't want to *hurt* him.

Driven to set things right, Mark got up and followed him out of the hall.

"Dean." Mark jogged to catch him up, as his schoolmate turned down the corridor.

Dean ignored him, his head low as he carried on.

As he drew close, Mark tugged on his arm, eventually getting Dean to stop. "I'm sorry. We're all sorry, we get carried away sometimes." Mark said, knowing it wasn't an excuse.

"Good that one of you deigned to apologise for once." Dean replied, his haughty tone lacking his usual confidence. He gave a dramatic sigh. "You guys have it so freakin' easy, you don't know how hellish high school is for the rest of us."

"Easy?" Mark choked. What part of the last few months had been easy? With the mob baying for his blood, and the threat of expulsion still ringing in his ears.

"You're the popular, exciting ones." Dean said, waving his arm expressively.

"What?" Mark was fairly sure having three friends in this school didn't make him popular.

"You've always been the witch, and Harry's always been the funny one girls are crushing on. It's like the whole world revolves around you. And now you've got the gorgeous footballer god in your exclusive clique, when I try so hard to be accepted..." Dean bit his lip, and gave a resigned shrug. "Y'know what, forget it. Please, of all people, I don't want *you* to be nice to me. Be mean, be a bastard, just don't be *nice*."

Dean turned on his heel and practically fled down the corridor, leaving Mark somewhat dazed.

So much for trying to do the right thing. He needed some sort of translator to figure out what Dean was saying.

As Mark sighed and turned away, he glimpsed movement through the window. Michelle and her friends were heading for the old bike shed. Snorting at the cliché, Mark headed outside.

The old bike shed was a dilapidated husk, with a leaky roof and old, rusty bars. Everyone who cycled used the new shed, that was much closer to the school.

The benefit of the old one, was it couldn't be seen clearly from any of the buildings, making it ideal for the smokers.

As he drew close, Mark could smell the acrid scent of stale cigarettes.

Michelle was sitting with three other students, her sleek London look fading back into the scruffy norm of a Tealford student.

Sensing his focus, Michelle turned to look at Mark with a withering gaze. Her friends followed suit, and Mark was the target of their silent disdain.

"Hi, I was checking... um..." His confidence trickled away, and he forgot what he was going to say.

Michelle handed her cigarette to the other girl in the group, and pushed off the wall.

"Couldn't you leave me in peace?" She hissed.

"Nanna asked me to keep an eye on you. I didn't see you at dinner." Mark replied, then lowered his voice. "If you need money for food..."

Michelle scowled. "I don't need your charity. Besides, you're too late; Nanna gave me a tenner this morning. I'm gonna pay her back, I don't need nobody."

"OK, sorry." Mark held up his hands defensively. His eyes drifted to her companions – all typical troublemakers. "Is it a good idea, hanging out with those guys? You've worked so hard to leave your darkness behind."

Michelle's already pale complexion blanched further. "You're seriously gonna pass judgement on my friends? Are they not good enough?"

"No, I didn't mean-"

"You don't know shit, Mark." Michelle balled her hands into fists and stepped menacingly close. "They might not be model students, but they're *good* people. The only dangerous one is *me*."

Mark stared at her for a minute, awkwardly aware of their audience.

"Sorry, I didn't mean to slate your friends. I just..." Mark quailed. "We've tried so hard to fix you-"

"Fix me?" Michelle echoed. "*Fix me*? I'm a dark magic addict, from a broken home. I'm never going to be *fixed*. I'm never going to be sunshine and rainbows, so don't judge me against what you consider normal."

"I didn't mean it like that." Mark tried, feebly.

"Then what did you mean?" Michelle demanded.

"Fine, I've gotten used to having you around, and I don't wanna lose you." Mark said in a rush, feeling increasingly uncomfortable. "I'll see you at home."

Having shocked Michelle into silence, Mark turned and rushed back to school, in time for the bell.

"Still not your friend." Came Michelle's voice.

Chapter Six

After school the next day, instead of heading home on the bus, Mark made his way to Tealford College. Mark would be coming here as an official student in September, to do his A Levels. The brochure described it as 'Art Deco', which really translated into big, unattractive block buildings.

Mark had been there several times to tour the campus before making his 'decision' about his future. Technically, he did have the choice of going to other colleges, but they were a pain in the arse to travel to. Being miles from anywhere else, 99% of Tealford High School students ended up in Tealford College.

Some of those college students watched Mark cross the campus, sniggering at his school uniform, as if they hadn't just shed it themselves twelve measly months ago.

Mark ignored them, and made his way to the History department, where he found Danny in one of the bright, airy rooms.

Mark had half-expected Danny to be wearing a tweed jacket as part of his professor-wardrobe. Mark was somewhat disappointed, as Danny was wearing a simple pink shirt with the sleeves rolled back. Perhaps it was too hot for tweed.

Danny was packing a few things into his briefcase, and looked up as Mark knocked.

"Mark - to what do I owe this pleasure?" He asked.

"Oh, y'know, came to see how you're getting on." Mark said, with what he thought was a casual air.

Danny wasn't fooled. "Nice try. What do you want?"

"Robert came to my house last night." Mark blurted out. "He wants to use my friendship with Silvaticus, to get rid of those hell beasts."

"So, you're here for Silvaticus." Danny narrowed his eyes suspiciously. "Figures."

"I came to see you, too." Mark added weakly. "I'd appreciate your opinion. Can I trust Silvaticus to help me?"

Danny snorted. "I've never been very popular, but people coming to see the demon, instead of me? That's a new low."

"I'm your friend, too." Mark insisted.

"Really? Then it must be a new development that I'm not aware of." Danny replied airily.

Mark bit his tongue, reminding himself that he needed Danny's help. It was so tempting to snap at the arrogant git. No wonder he didn't have many friends.

"Look, I'm glad you came, I wanted to talk to you..." Danny took a deep breath. "Since Silvaticus joined me... his experience of life is so dizzyingly broad; I fear that I may have come across as ignorant and possibly insensitive on several occasions." Danny's gaze was fixed resolutely on his desk, his usual confidence wavering before Mark's eyes.

Mark tried to get to the bottom of Danny's rambling. "Are you... apologising?"

"Well, you know, if you want to call it that..." Danny mumbled. "I now realise that some of my previous comments could be construed as hurtful. That was never my intention..."

Mark paused, waiting for the actual words 'I am sorry', but he realised this was the closest to an apology Danny could probably offer. "Thank you, I appreciate it. I'm grateful that Silvaticus is proving educational. Do you think I can trust him?"

Danny sighed, looking relieved. "He seems to be a man – or demon, rather – of his word. As far as demons go, I believe you can trust him."

Mark nodded. "Can I please speak to him?"

Mark didn't realise how much nervous energy was rolling off Danny, until it all stilled. In comparison, Silvaticus was a deep well of power, calm and resonant.

The demon turned his black eyes on Mark, making his resolve stutter. "Well met, Mark."

"Hi Silvaticus, I-" Mark broke off before he repeated himself. "Did you hear what I said to Danny? I'm not sure where the lines are drawn between you two..."

Silvaticus closed his eyes and nodded gently. "Danny is still learning the ways of a host. I give him complete privacy, unless he invites me to watch and listen. He has yet to gain confidence in his own authority over me... I heard what you had to say."

"Um... I didn't mean to question my trust in you..." Mark said, a hot blush creeping up his neck. "Especially after you saved us in London."

"I may be a creature of honour, but I am still a demon. I understand your wariness."

Mark swallowed nervously. "Can you help?"

"I can't believe things have evolved, so that *I* would help *Robert*."

Mark gave a sigh. "I can relate. I'm trying not to see how it will benefit Robert. Those hell beasts are still roaming the countryside, a threat to people and animals." Mark recalled how they'd chased him down, even though he wasn't their official target. He remembered the beasts breathing down his neck and flooding him with fear… "We need to get rid of them. I suppose if it's beyond your abilities, I could always ask the coven…"

Silvaticus didn't rise to Mark's ribbing, and when he spoke it was with his usual, cool logic. "Your coven might be able to deal with the beast attacks, but it is simply reacting to the symptoms. Hell beasts are demon business, and a demon needs to stop the source."

"Will you be the demon that stops them?" Mark asked, pressing the point.

"Indeed." Silvaticus said, with another slow nod. "We shall go to the demon realm immediately."

"We?" Mark blinked in surprise. "*Now*?"

Silvaticus looked him up and down. "I think it would be an exercise of *trust*, for you to come with me. And did you have a better time in mind?"

"No, I…" Mark shook his head. "What's it like? Will it be safe?"

"It will be safe, as long as you stay with me." Silvaticus raised his hand, resting it on Mark's bare arm. "*Síþwegas.*"

"No-"

There was a flash of blinding light, and the classroom vanished into the dark red nothingness of the demon road. The silence was oppressive, and Mark wondered if the whole of the demon realm was like this.

The seconds stretched on forever, but eventually there was another flash of light.

Mark blinked, his eyes still burning. "You can't just drag me into another realm!"

"I am perfectly capable of bringing others with me." Silvaticus replied, frowning at the lad's outburst.

"I didn't mean... ugh." Mark sighed. Were there any rules, or societal expectations for this? "Can you please ask my permission, next time?"

"Very well." Silvaticus replied, looking almost bemused.

"Nanna is gonna kill me." Mark muttered, remembering his promise not to do anything rash without notifying her. He pulled out his phone, and was not surprised to see it had no signal.

Oh well, since he was here, he might as well make the most of it. Mark took a long look at the surroundings, his excitement bubbling that he was getting his first glimpse at a new reality.

The sky was grey, and gave the weak light of twilight, with no sun or moon hovering above. The land rolled away in gentle hills covered in purple heather, reminding Mark of the moors in late summer.

Mark could see stone columns, marking where their gate had opened. A well-worn gravel track led away, into the shadows of the hills.

There was something in the atmosphere, or in the ground itself, that made Mark wary. The same way his instincts cried danger every time Robert was close. Danger, and power…

Out of habit, Mark tried to call on his magic, but it didn't respond. He closed his eyes and tried to create a simple circle, but there was nothing. "My magic doesn't work!"

"Your magic is fuelled by nature. There is nothing natural here." Silvaticus said, with his usual calm. "Don't worry, you won't need it if you stick close to me."

"Oh, how reassuring…" Mark replied, a cold sweat breaking out on his neck, at the thought of going through the demon realm defenceless.

"We need to travel to the gael. It is an hour's ride away." Silvaticus said, walking away from the stone columns.

"An hour's ride?" Mark echoed, unable to see any form of transport in the vicinity. In fact, there didn't seem to be another living creature as far as his eyes could see.

Silvaticus knelt down, placing his hand on the damp soil. "*Mēaras.*"

Mark sensed the dark magic flow between the demon and the land, the strength of it snatched the breath out of Mark's chest.

The ground beneath his feet rumbled, and Mark staggered closer to Silvaticus, hoping the demon would keep his promise of safety.

The heather and scrub grass bubbled up, into a living mound. Ready to burst, the greenery peeled away to leave a bone-pale shifting mass beneath it.

"What the hell is that?" Mark gasped.

"Transport." Silvaticus replied calmly.

There was more movement, as bulky, disjointed limbs clambered out of the ground.

Mark held his breath, as he saw two stone horses. They stood obediently, waiting for commands from their creator.

"Wow." Mark stepped closer to them, admiring the spell. It was definitely magic beyond his skills.

"We don't have cars in this realm. The demon road is the fastest way to travel, but there are limited gates on this side." Silvaticus said, leaping on the broad back of the nearest beast, with surprising agility.

Mark tried to follow suit, vaulting onto the second horse, but he had to shuffle inelegantly to finish the climb. Finally astride, Mark placed his hand on the horse, expecting it to be soft and warm, like the real thing; but the cold rock dug into his flesh.

"Do you remember how to get to this jail?" Mark asked, trying to find a comfortable position. "It's been a while since you've been free to roam."

Silvaticus gazed out at the countryside, taking a moment to consider Mark's question. "The demon realm stays the same. They don't like change."

Mark chewed his lip. "There's not a funny time difference, like a fae world? I'm not gonna return to Tealford fifty years from now?"

"Faeries are tricksters, you would do well not to stumble into their realm." Silvaticus replied. "An hour here, is the same as an hour in your world; demons just have a different concept of time. Perhaps as a result of immortality."

"Oh, that's good – wait, faeries are real?" Mark grinned. He'd only been looking for a mythical comparison, he didn't expect them to be real.

Silvaticus nodded his head once. "Let us proceed."

The horses sprang into action. Mark jolted with surprise, and clung onto his beast's side. As it settled into a steady canter, he managed to pull himself upright again. The stone horse's rhythm was surprisingly smooth, but Mark knew that his thighs would still be bruised to hell from going bareback.

The horses covered the ground swiftly, never tiring, or losing focus on their destination. As they both obeyed Silvaticus, and needed no further aids from Mark, he took the opportunity to take in the sights. The hills were gentle and covered in purple heather, and the background remained so steady, it became quite unnerving.

"Is all of the demon realm like this?" Mark asked, unable to explain why the unchanging scenery was so unsettling.

"No, this is simply the in-between. It belongs to no demon, so must suit all. A land without sun, without moon; frozen in perpetual dusk." Silvaticus replied, without looking his way. "We will move into the Brimcliff Duchy soon."

As far as Mark could see, the empty land went on for miles, stretching out as far as the eye could see. Mark didn't see it changing within the hour Silvaticus insisted it would take to ride to the jail. He didn't see it changing for ten hours, or a day.

"Wh-" Mark's question broke off, as he saw a ripple in the air. "What's that?"

Silvaticus didn't answer, and the horses didn't change their pace.

The shimmer in the air grew closer. Mark held his breath as it rippled and folded over them. The unfamiliar magic licked across his skin, making him shiver.

The temperature dropped 10 degrees, and Mark could taste salt in the air. The rolling moors dissolved into greyness. The mossy grass turned into stone and shrivelled bushes that lay dark against the ground.

The gentle background was replaced by harsh cliffs and sudden drops. A violent sea rolled and crashed against the rocky shore, cold spray filtering through the air.

There was life – for the first time, Mark saw living creatures in the demon realm.

Giant lizard beasts swarmed up and down the cliffs, their deadly claws digging into the sheer stone faces. Their cries bird-like screeches that split the air.

There were dark buildings blending into the shadowy background, the windows filled with green light. People milled through the narrow, winding streets.

As the horses carried them closer, Mark could see the people were not quite human. Despite walking on two feet, some had scales for skin, and wide, slit-shaped eyes, that fixed on the travellers. Another pair were covered in brown hair, that was so sleek, it looked wet. Others looked human enough, but were pale and lifeless, and didn't even notice that strangers were near.

"What are they?" Mark asked quietly, when the crowd had grown so thick, the horses had to slow to a walk.

"There are a lot of demons in this Duchy that descend from sea serpents." Silvaticus cast a disinterested glance at the reptilians, before turning his gaze to the hairy ones. "Then there's selkies. One of the few demons that can move between realms without a human host. They can choose to look human, but that skill is wasted down here."

"What about the pasty-looking ones?"

"Slaves." Silvaticus remarked, in his usual calm manner. "People that have sold their souls to one demon or another."

"You have *slaves*?" Mark gasped.

"They are currency for demons – the more souls bound to them, the more powerful they are." Silvaticus returned his eyes to the road. "The usual contract is ninety-nine years of servitude, after a person's death. Many think it is a fair deal, for whatever the demon promises – wealth, health, good fortune..."

Mark recalled the vision he'd seen of Damian's father, who had been so desperate to turn his life around, that he had been willing to sell his soul. Unfortunately, the demon he'd chosen wasn't interested in *his* soul; instead Robert wanted to possess his son.

"Do you have any slaves?" Mark asked.

Silvaticus gave a slow shake of his head. "No. Not for a long time. It has been more than a thousand years since I turned my back on the politics of the demon realm. I found a way to exist in your world, to have purpose."

"Possessing innocent people."

"I have never possessed a man or woman who did not welcome it. Life is bitter enough, without an ungrateful host."

"Damian accepted Robert. It was under duress, but technically willing." Mark argued.

"True. Robert has never understood the benefits of a symbiotic partnership, so he will never be as strong as I am." Silvaticus explained.

Mark frowned, after Robert's comments about working with Damian, he wasn't so sure. They made their way to the rocky shore, where a rickety-looking jetty stood against the crashing waves.

Silvaticus dismounted, and Mark followed suit. The two stone horses stood completely immobile, waiting for their master to return.

Mark stood idly while Silvaticus arranged for a boat, with a scale-skinned boatman.

"Where are we going?" Mark asked quietly.

"The Brimcliff Prison is offshore. That is the source of the hell beasts."

Mark gazed at the little boat warily. It looked like one small wave would decimate it, shattering the flimsy panels of wood, and dropping its passengers to the depths. "Are you sure this will hold us?"

Silvaticus stepped into the boat, unworried. "You are thinking with human rules and limitations, Mark. Do you really think that a demon boat, in a demon sea, will be kept afloat by physics?"

Not entirely comforted by Silvaticus' logic, Mark stepped into the boat gingerly, gritting his teeth and ready for the whole thing to go under. Miraculously, it stayed afloat, and strangely level against the crashing waves.

The boatman stood at the back of the boat, holding a rudder with a scaly hand. With nothing more than magic, the boat propelled forwards, into the open sea.

Mark gripped the side of the boat tightly, cold spray soaking through his school uniform. He grit his teeth against the shivers, it was quite the contrast to the pleasant Yorkshire summer he'd left behind.

Mark spotted what he thought was a lonely hunk of rock, jutting out of the sea, and towering over the surrounding waves. As they drew closer, he realised that it was much bigger than he'd first thought. It was a massive monolith of rock, which cast everything to shadow around it.

The boatman steered to one corner. Mark worried they were going to crash into the stone wall, but when they got close, the boat swerved down a narrow, hidden channel. They were plunged into darkness, with a single green light drawing them ahead.

They finally reached a small dock, and Mark was grateful to be on solid ground again.

A figure moved out of the shadows next to them. It was as tall as Mark, and vaguely human-shaped. It looked like it was made from grey clay, and the featureless form wore a simple tunic and a sharp sword at its hip. The creature turned its eyeless face towards them.

"We are here to see the Governor." Silvaticus said.

The creature nodded, and unlocked a steel gate. It stood aside to let them pass.

Silvaticus stepped into the dark corridor beyond, he hesitated briefly, as though getting his bearings, then led on. Mark jumped after him, feeling nowhere near as calm as his companion.

"What was that?" Mark asked.

"A golem." Silvaticus replied. "Most of the guards are golems, creatures made of clay and magic. They do not tire, and they cannot be deceived."

Mark stuck close to Silvaticus' side, as they moved through the prison. The thick rock walls of the prison blocked out the sound of the wild seas outside, making the sounds inside the prison so much clearer. There were moans, squawks and whimpering. Mark stamped down the impulse to run back to the exit.

As they passed deeper into the prison, they started to pass the cells. Some had solid walls, others were separated by iron bars. The cells were everywhere, along each side, in the ceiling and even in the floor. The ones that were occupied had a variety of demons and creatures that Mark couldn't describe. For all their vast physical differences, they all had the same glassy stare, a look of pain and broken wills that crushed Mark's heart.

They eventually stopped at a large oak door, which Silvaticus knocked sharply on.

The door swung open to reveal a large office, with books and scrolls filling the walls and piles on the floor. There was a fireplace lit with that strange green fire, which didn't give out much warmth.

Behind a table was a creature that was official-looking compared to the golem guards that Mark had spied. They had eyes and ears, and seaweed-coloured hair that lay flat and lank. Several limbs curled like tentacles from a rather thick body.

"Silvaticus, how good to see you again. What an interesting choice for your new host." The creature announced loudly. Her dark eyes moved to Mark. "And what's this, a human? Alive?"

The creature licked its lips, her nearest tentacle moving towards Mark with a steady determination.

"A witch. He's under my protection, Governor." Silvaticus said firmly.

The tentacle stopped its approach, but was slow to retract. "Well, if you ever tire of your toy…"

"Governor, we are here to discuss the cessation of the hell beasts chasing the demon currently known as Robert."

The Governor's attention snapped back to Silvaticus, her brow creasing in what Mark assumed was a frown. "*You* want us to stop hunting *him*? After everything he's done to you and your hosts?"

"I have not forgiven him," Silvaticus confirmed. "But the hell beasts are causing trouble for many innocent humans. They need to be removed."

"Very well, that is your prerogative..." The Governor moved away from the desk, her body rippling instead of walking.

A wide door opened, and Mark felt a familiar overwhelming sense of anger and pain. In the dull light, he could just make out the shapes of hell beasts. Canine in appearance, they looked as insubstantial as shadows. As the Governor moved towards them, they bared their teeth and backed away, whining and whimpering, expecting more pain.

The Governor returned, with a red rag wrapped in a tentacle. "It is done." She said, throwing the material towards them.

Mark snatched it out of the air, unfolding what turned out to be a Topman jumper. He felt a dirty shiver run up his spine, which had nothing to do with the cold. This was Damian's, it had to be.

Mark twisted it in his hands, trying to calm his temper. What the hell were they doing with Damian's jumper? How did they get it? Mark hated the idea of any of these monsters getting close to his boyfriend.

"You have my thanks." Silvaticus said, bowing his head towards the Governor.

When Silvaticus moved to the door to exit, Mark snapped out of his revery. He hurried to keep up, not wanting to be left alone in a demon prison.

As they left the Governor's room, Mark could feel the creature's eyes fixed on him with an unsettling, possessive gaze.

"This is Damian's." Mark snapped, brandishing the jumper in Silvaticus' face.

"Like your hunting hounds at home, they benefit from having an item belonging to their quarry." Silvaticus explained in his usual calm tone, unruffled by Mark's actions.

"Where did they even get it?"

"I believe they retrieved it from the boy's house in London."

Mark shivered, he'd been to Damian's London house with Harry and Sarah. There had been signs of someone breaking in before they'd gotten there. Mark had assumed that it was Damian, or local thugs; it made his blood run cold to think a demon could have been in the house at the same time as them.

Mark felt a little relief that the demon-hunters hadn't been near Yorkshire. He couldn't bear the idea of Damian rotting away behind these bars. "Is this the prison Robert escaped from?"

"It is."

Mark waited, but Silvaticus didn't provide any more information. "And? How did he do it?"

Silvaticus gave him a cool glance. "I do not know, and any guess would be mere speculation."

Mark rolled his eyes at the demon's complete lack of curiosity. Silvaticus and his host Danny were a match made in heaven.

Mark noticed the temperature drop, and the dank smell of the prison became a little fresher, as they made their way to the little dock. The golem guard let them out of the bolted door, and Mark could see that the scaled boatman was waiting for them.

"Is this the only way out of the prison?" Mark asked. He couldn't imagine Robert had arranged for a boat to pick him up during his break-out.

"It is." Silvaticus confirmed. "Many have died trying to swim these seas."

As the scaled boatman steered them back out to sea, Mark stood quietly, thoughts crashing through his head, like the violent waves surrounding them. The demons hadn't just been trying to capture Robert, they'd been hunting *Damian*, too.

After visiting the demon prison, Mark wouldn't even wish incarceration on his worst enemy; but to imagine that Damian could be locked up alongside Robert…

"Damian can never end up here. Do what you want with Robert, but Damian goes free." He insisted, shouting against the crashing waves and salty air.

Silvaticus took a moment, taking in his request, then tilted his head in agreement. "I will not harm the boy, Damian. I swear it."

When they got back to shore, the two stone horses were still standing with their heads erect, waiting for their master's command.

Mark clambered back aboard, wincing at the bruises that had already formed on his thighs. What he wouldn't give for a real horse right now, especially a fat, comfortable one like his Nanna's cob. In fact, he'd even prefer to travel in Nanna's Land Rover... or maybe not.

They started to make their way through the seaside town, the dark houses low-slung and clinging to the rocky terrain. Amongst the constant grey and green, Mark spotted a halo of blonde hair, framing an angelic face. There was a girl in a pale blue sundress, in the middle of a demon village. She looked to be about his age, and when she turned to look his way, her bright blue eyes pierced his soul.

"Who's that?" He asked.

Silvaticus glanced over, for once looking irritated by Mark's question. "A demon. She's harmless enough. Leave her be, she's a bit of a pest."

Mark's horse continued down the path that Silvaticus chose, moving swiftly inland. Mark could feel the blonde demon's eyes still fixed on him, long after she disappeared behind the crowd.

The journey back was uneventful. When they reached the boundary of the Brimcliff Duchy, Mark thought he was ready for the sudden change of scenery, but it still made his head spin. The grey rocks shifted jarringly into purple heather.

Despite their mission having taken several hours, nothing had altered in the moors. Silvaticus had warned him that this in-between place was frozen in time, Mark was still struck by how unsettling it was. They travelled back in silence, and Mark was relieved to see the stone pillars that marked the demon gate.

As soon as they dismounted, the horses crumbled, no longer held together by Silvaticus' spell. They were just rubble and dust, half-hidden beneath the heather.

Mark took one last look at the demon realm, then grabbed Silvaticus' arm.

Chapter Seven

The first of May was supposed to herald the start of summer, so in true British fashion, the day dawned cold and grey. Heavy clouds threatened rain, and a chill wind blew across the hills.

Never put off by such a thing, Mark and his family headed into Tealford. Every year a small travelling fair came through for the first week of May. It might not be much compared to a real fairground, but it was a highlight for everyone at Tealford, and Mark had many happy memories as a child.

They all piled into the car, and Mark's Dad drove into town, navigating the queuing traffic to find a place to park.

Mark recognised other students from school, and other witches from the coven milling through the crowd, enjoying May Day with their families.

Mark's own family poured out of the car, and made slow progress towards the fair. Every couple of steps, they were stopped by friends and acquaintances. People that chatted and laughed with Mark's parents, or begged for a few minutes of Nanna's time.

Leaving the adults to do their socialising, Mark found himself walking ahead with Michelle. Until she too came across some friends.

Michelle hesitated, looking awkwardly back at Mark. "You're welcome to... um." She gestured vaguely in the direction of her friends.

"Thanks, but I'm meeting Damian." Mark replied, surprised that Michelle would invite him along.

"Good, not your friend." She said, before disappearing swiftly.

Mark checked his phone, and headed to the picnic benches where Damian was waiting for him.

His boyfriend was perched on one of the benches, looking as fashionable as ever, with his skinny jeans and grey jacket. Damian looked up as Mark approached, a pinched look on his face.

"I thought it was supposed to be summer." Damian jumped up from the bench, shoving his hands deep into his pockets. "Why isn't it warm yet?"

Mark grinned at his reaction. "I warned you..."

"No, you warned me that winter was cold, you never told me about the rest of the year."

"Then we'll have to warm you up." Mark linked arms with Damian, and steered him towards the fair.

"Um, in a PG, public-friendly walk. Not anything... amorous."

"How disappointing." Damian replied playfully. His bright blue eyes roved over the fairground.

The rides were in full swing, the usual array of spinning arms and strapped-in people screaming in delight. There were smaller stands, with games; and delicious-smelling greasy food.

The way that Damian drank it all in seemed full of innocent curiosity.

"Did you go to many of these in London?"

Damian shook his head. "No, my parents never took me when I was a kid. The fairs were never local to us, and always real crowded. This is kinda nice. Do you have any advice?"

"Yeah, don't trip over the wires." Mark blushed at his own mistake. "And if you want to win a goldfish, leave it 'til last – you don't wanna take it on the Twister with you."

Damian grinned and dragged Mark into the fairground, weaving through the crowd to the nearest ride. They found Harry and Sarah in the queue for the Waltzer, and jumped in the same car as them.

There were only a dozen rides to have a go on, and compared to the big fairgrounds, the queues were short. They managed to go on every ride twice.

Damian uploaded their group photos onto his Instagram, smiling at the memories made.

Mark had to admit that he was also enjoying spending a very simple and human day with his friends. No witches, no demons, no trouble. It was such a contrast to the demon realm, which was still etched into his senses. There it was quiet, full of foreboding and cold on more than one front. Here, there was life and joy.

Mark couldn't help talking about his trip, but every time he mentioned the demon realm, his friends got an apprehensive look on their faces. Mark didn't know if they were worried about the world being bigger than they thought; or they were simply bored from Mark's repeated stories.

Despite their stomachs still being tied in knots from being spun in every possible direction over the last few hours, they drifted back to have dinner with Mark's family; for big greasy burgers and burning hot chips.

Everyone fell silent as a very attractive guy made a beeline for Nanna. He was tall, with muscled arms from a lifetime of wrestling horses. His once-dark hair had thick streaks of grey, and there were deep laughter lines etched into his skin; but Mark had to admit he was good-looking for an older guy.

Nanna, looking more than a little smug, made introductions between Derek and her family. When his back was turned, Mark's Mum gave Nanna an embarrassing high five. His Dad... looked less than pleased.

"Just imagine, he might be your new grandpa... *you're gonna have a hot grandpa.*" Michelle nudged Mark's side and laughed.

The sound was so innocent and honest, that Mark paused. He was so used to Michelle's sarcasm and the cruel side of her humour; this was an interesting development.

Since his grandad had died, this was the first man to earn Nanna's affection, and Mark couldn't help sneaking looks at him. To say he was meeting her family and friends for the first time, Derek seemed very relaxed, and had a calm confidence that just seemed to draw people's attention. Mark could see why he'd been causing such a buzz.

Everyone was so busy cooing over the newcomer, that when a bitter voice piped up, it cut through the pleasant atmosphere.

"What is *he* doing here?"

Mark turned at the same time as his family, to spy a woman he vaguely recognised. Behind her were some other ladies, and their kids, looking at them spitefully. He wondered why she was getting upset over Nanna's new boyfriend...

"That boy is dangerous. Last time he was in a crowd, he nearly killed a restaurant full of people, and a house full of students. How dare you bring him out with normal people?"

Mark's heart dropped, realising that Derek wasn't the cause of the upset. Had it been too much to hope that the rest of Tealford had forgotten the little demon incidents a few months ago?

Before Mark could defend himself, Nanna had already responded.

"Normal? What do you know about normal, Daphne?"

The woman's thin mouth pursed further. "We all know that he used magic to hurt people."

"You *know*? What a relief." Nanna rolled her eyes. "Your sources are faulty; my grandson has saved your muggle arses on more than one occasion."

Daphne sniffed, pulling her handbag defensively in front of her. "You witches think you're all above the law. My niece was at the restaurant, she saw everything."

"And your niece just happens to be adept at recognising light and dark magic at work? How lucky." Nanna replied, her voice dripping with sarcasm. "Now, if you and your groupies will please move on, we were enjoying a family day out."

Nanna turned away, but Daphne wasn't done. She looked furious at being dismissed, and stepped forward.

Mark felt magic shimmer in the air, a thick barrier blocking Daphne from the family. The woman's anger turned to shock as she opened her mouth, and nothing but a strangled cry came out.

"Didn't you learn – if you can't say anything nice, don't say anything at all." Nanna replied coolly, looking over her shoulder at Daphne.

The woman gave a feline hiss, but quickly looked cowed, her arrogant posture crumbling.

"Your voice will come back on one condition – you stop spreading lies about my grandson. If you break this spell, there is nothing we can do to give you your voice back." Nanna warned.

Mark could sense Nanna's magic weave over the other woman, and settle like a second skin. He was in awe again, over her skill and strength.

"Understood?" Nanna demanded.

"Yes." Daphne replied, her voice high-pitched, but human.

Daphne looked like she was going to say something more, but thought better of it. She hiked her handbag onto her shoulder, and marched off, with her followers in tow.

Used to Nanna's behaviour, Mark's family were unphased by her little demonstration.

Newcomer Derek looked surprised. He gave a little cough. "So the 'witch' thing isn't just a title, it's real?"

"Yes." Nanna replied, actually blushing. "I won't be offended if it's something you can't handle."

Derek cocked his head, reassessing whatever he thought he knew about magic. "Don't worry, you can't scare me off that easily."

Nanna smiled, accepting the challenge.

Mark chewed his lip, as a kid, he'd always been blind to the little spells Nanna cast; but now he'd learnt a lot. He thought that included being responsible. "Nanna, was that really wise?"

"It was worth it. She might act all anti-witch, but Daphne tried to join the coven in the nineties." Nanna waved her hand dismissively.

"What?" Mark frowned, finding it impossible to imagine that stuck up woman being part of his coven.

"Daphne didn't have the right attitude. She thought she could jump straight into the big spells, and thought she'd be all that. She gave up when she realised how much work it would be." Nanna reeled off, then glanced down at her two students. "Of course, magic is an important responsibility, and shouldn't be taken lightly, or used frivolously."

"Except when showing off to bullies." Mark teased.

"I did not 'show off'." Nanna argued. "I quickly educated them to my superior skills with a carefully-calculated demonstration. The fact that they were impressed shows they had good sense."

Mark's laugh was quickly cut short.

"Don't you dare mention you went to the demon realm in front of that hag." Nanna warned. "I know you're excited about your adventure, but it'll only add fuel to her fire."

Nanna behaved herself for the rest of the day.

Mark and his family hung out at the fairground for a few more hours, until the rain started. A couple of drops soon turned into a heavy shower, that chased them all to find shelter, laughing at the 'summer' weather.

Mark found himself pressed closely to Damian, as they huddled under the nearest shop awning. His fingers curled around his boyfriend's gloved hand.

"Are you coming round to ours for Beltane festivities?" Mark asked quietly.

Damian frowned, trying to remember what Mark had told him about the pagan calendar. "That's one of the fire festivals, right?"

"Yeah, we try and have a bonfire to celebrate, but I think today is a bit of a wash-out." Mark glanced at the pouring rain which didn't look like it was going to lighten up. "There will still be a barbecue at my house, if you fancy more burgers?"

Damian squeezed his hand. "Spend the rest of the day with you? Yeah, I'm up for that."

Chapter Eight

That afternoon, there was quite the crowd at Mark's house. Damian's Aunt Maggie and her girlfriend arrived early; followed by Denise and other witches from the coven piling in.

It wasn't quite the turn-out that the bonfires brought, with the local families taking advantage of the parties; but it was fairly decent. The adults enjoying an excuse to let their hair down.

Unfortunately, Harry and Sarah couldn't make it due to prior family commitments. Mark kicked himself, that he'd forgotten to invite them until the last minute. He kept forgetting his friends didn't know the witchy calendar by heart.

In typical British-barbecue style, Mark's Dad had already erected the gazebo over the grill, that would keep the worst of the rain away; and he had his cagoule for the trips to the house.

"Can't you do something witchy to send the rain away?" Derek the farrier asked Nanna, with an honest curiosity.

"No, it's not worth the risk. We can push the rain away for a few hours, but the repercussion could be a drought or a flood." Nanna reeled off, discussing her own version of the weather. "Elemental magic is simple, but strong. It's easy to knock them out of balance."

Mark could attest to that. He recalled the Thames flooding, as a backlash to his air spell, a couple of months ago. The water had rushed over them with such a wild force, nothing could stop it. At the time, it had slowed down the Dark witches chasing them, but the raw power still made Mark shiver.

"How about I take a beer out to Michael, and see if there's anything I can do to help?" Derek offered. "I've got a bit of experience stoking reluctant fires in the rain."

There was a titter of polite laughter at his joke. Mark didn't know if forge-skills transferred to working a barbecue, but Derek scooped up a beer and dashed outside, braving the rain.

Mark had to bite his lip to stop from laughing at his Dad's reaction. He scowled at the handsome man that was dating his mother.

Mark realised that working the barbecue was one of the traditionally-accepted male-bonding rituals. All it needed was an Attenborough narration... 'here we see the middle-aged males tentatively test the water and the social hierarchy. The one who gets the fire to work will inevitably win the alpha role, and the respect of his clan...'

Mark snorted at the internal dialogue, getting confused looks from Damian and Michelle. He shook his head, not wanting to share how weird his thoughts were.

Everyone's attention less-than-subtly shifted to Derek as he made his way back to the house. The summer rain soaked through his shirt to show his still-fit physique and corded muscles.

"You're totally getting a hot grandpa." Michelle whispered to Mark, before turning to Derek. "So, Derek, what are your intentions with our Nanna? If that's not too weird to ask?"

Derek looked surprised at the ambush, but his smile seemed genuine enough. "That's not weird, you're her grandkids, of course you care what happens in her life."

"Oh, I'm not her granddaughter."

"Oh, that's a little weird then." Derek looked nonplussed, but laughed. "We're dating, and I hope to continue dating for as long as I'm here. I know she's the big matriarch of this place, and I'm lucky she wants to spend time with me."

"Just remember – if you hurt her, we know all the curses under the sun." Michelle winked. "You may continue."

Not sure if Michelle was joking, Derek gave another little laugh, before hurrying back to the adults.

"Aw, look at you getting all protective." Mark grinned. "You're really part of the good-witch coven now."

Whereas Michelle's previous reactions had been to violently deny light magic, and threaten them all demon-fuelled pain, she now just shrugged. "Meh, they'll be lucky to have me."

The first round of barbecued meat made its way inside, and the house became a hive of activity, as everyone helped themselves to what they liked best. As the adults had another beer and seemed to take up every available space downstairs, Mark carried his plate upstairs, trailed by Damian and Michelle.

"Huh, your room's bigger than mine." Michelle commented, snatching up the remote and immediately flicking through the options on Mark's TV.

Mark chuckled at her comment, his brief jealousy of sharing the house with Michelle had long-since faded, but he wondered what would happen in the end. Michelle seemed happy here, but once she recovered from her stint with dark magic would she go back to her parents' house?

Except for the time Michelle had confessed that she'd been adopted, they'd never spoken about her parents. It had become an unwritten rule between them. The fact that her parents hadn't tried to see her in all the time Michelle had lived here didn't cast them in a great light.

Mark and Damian got comfortable on Mark's bed, and Michelle curled into the big cushions of the cosy armchair.

Michelle had picked Supernatural, which made Mark snort.

"Don't we have enough demons in real life?"

It was good to get distracted by fantasy over real drama for a while. Mark played waiter and made sure his friends had a steady supply of pop. It was nice to chat about normal stuff, too; as they discussed Dean's party and Harry's upcoming performance.

Michelle streamed a video from Instagram, and they all got to relive Harry's last set.

"He's so good." Damian sighed.

"He is." Mark confirmed, then gave Damian a nudge with his elbow. "Just wait 'til you see him live."

A cute blush crept across Damian's face. "It's a date."

With his eyes cast downwards, Mark noticed how pale Damian's eyelashes looked, against his tanned summer skin. When Damian looked back up, his blue eyes were all the more alive-

A cushion thunked against the wall by Mark's head.

"Ugh, you two need to stop looking at each other like that, I'm gonna hurl." Michelle announced.

"He's my boyfriend, it's allowed." Mark said, embarrassed that he'd been caught showing his feelings so transparently. He threw the cushion back at Michelle in retaliation.

"Yeah, but the problem is that *your* boyfriend looks exactly like *my* ex-boyfriend." Michelle argued. "Made worse by the fact my ex now has a thing for you."

"What?" Damian sat straighter. "What has Robert done now?"

"Nowt." Mark insisted.

"Nowt?" Michelle snorted. "He makes doe eyes at you every time he appears."

Mark squeezed his boyfriend's hand. "It's not like it sounds. He just runs a little hotter than the rest of us. He stops flirting when I ask him to. Mostly."

Damian pulled his hand away.

"Damian..."

"No, I don't blame you." Damian said, looking at Mark with pained eyes. "I hate that he can take over my body like that, and put you in this position. I have these black gaps in my memory; he could have done anything and I'm still powerless to stop him."

Mark remembered what Robert had said the last time he saw him, about Damian changing his mind about the demon. "You still want to stop him?"

"Of course I do!"

"We still don't even know why he's here." Mark said. "I don't trust how good Robert has been lately."

"He killed Eadric." Damian pointed out.

"*Indirectly*. It doesn't count."

Damian snorted. "I'd hate to see what you'd class as 'bad'."

"Any input Michelle?"

"I'm not exactly in his inner circle anymore." The goth girl shrugged. "He was always plotting, if we don't know what he's doing, that's how he's planned it. Robert thinks of *everything*."

"Do you have any access to his thoughts?" Mark asked Damian.

His boyfriend shook his head.

"He has some dark witches in Sheffield working for him, they might know something." Michelle suggested.

Mark snorted, remembering Edith and her followers threatening them with torture and death. "No thanks."

Michelle rolled her eyes. "They're not in Edith's level. Nowhere near. We could take them."

"I don't want to fight them." Mark said.

"What if Robert was there?" Damian asked, brightening up. "Some black contacts and they won't be able to see the difference."

Mark smiled at his boyfriend's idea. "Yeah, but they might feel the difference."

"What?"

"Robert brims with dark energy when he's in control." Mark explained. "I'm guessing even these mediocre witches can feel it."

"Huh." Damian looked unsettled again.

"Plus, they're all a bunch of sycophants." Michelle added. "They're so hooked on Robert's power, they'll be super annoying and we won't get any sense out of them, if they think he's there."

"So what do you suggest, Michelle?" Damian asked, his voice more stressed than normal.

"Me and Mark go as a couple of dark witches. They know me, it won't be suspicious."

"Michelle, are you sure it's a good idea for you to get involved with dark witches again?" Mark asked, worried that all their progress would be lost.

"It's just *dark witches*, not dark magic." Michelle said with a shrug and overly-casual attitude. "Unless a demon is fuelling their power, these witches aren't even strong enough to use dark spells."

"Fine, when do we go?"

"Well, now is as good a time as any."

"Now?" Damian groaned.

"Trust me, they'll all be gathered on Beltane." Michelle said. "It's perfect – they're weak anyways, but Mark and I are juiced on natural magic right now. Nowt can go wrong."

Mark shared a look with Damian, and his boyfriend shrugged in return. It sounded a harmless enough excursion.

"Fine, let's go."

"Uh, not dressed like that, you're not." Michelle stated, sneering at Mark's outfit. "Don't you have anything that doesn't make you look like a boy scout?"

Mark groaned, but decided to play along. Michelle knew the crowd that they wanted to blend into, and Mark would abide by her shining wisdom. He got up and rooted through his wardrobe. He pulled out a black t-shirt and black jeans, taking inspiration from Michelle's usual monochromatic get-up.

"Uh, privacy please?" He reminded her.

"Don't worry, you're not my type." Michelle said, with a rueful glance at Damian. She dutifully turned away so Mark could get changed.

Damian followed suit, politely turning away, although part of Mark wanted him to look.

Once Mark was dressed, he gestured to his all-black ensemble. "Better?"

Michelle took one look at his clothes and gave a harsh bark of laughter. "Now you look like the mysterious, yet inoffensive 'bad guy' from a teen soap."

Mark sighed, looking in the mirror. He could see what she meant, his clothes were all clean-cut and flattering. He was definitely in a brand-new costume. "I don't think I can pull this off."

"I'll be back in a min." Michelle said, ducking out of the room.

"I think you look good." Damian said, eyeing him appreciatively.

Mark's sense of style was amateurish next to Damian's, but it was still good to hear. "Thanks."

Taking advantage of their moment alone, Mark knelt on the bed next to Damian, and leant in for a kiss.

Damian responded with his usual soft eagerness, a shivering hesitation, as the intimate moment stretched on.

Mark yelped as something was thrown at his head. He looked round to see Michelle hovering in the doorway.

"Michelle, not cool."

"I thought we agreed you'd postpone the lovey-dovey stuff when I'm here."

"No, you agreed it. And you weren't here." Mark snapped, then glanced down at her missile, an over-sized black t-shirt. "This is a girl's top."

"It's unisex. Put it on, loser." Michelle replied. "I also brought some chains and some studded cuffs."

Mark groaned, but pulled the t-shirt on. It was well-worn, with fraying hems and the black more of a washed-out grey. He let Michelle add her accessories, pulling a face the whole time.

Michelle stepped back and admired her handiwork. "Well, now you've graduated to the inoffensive punk character in a teen drama. It's the best we're gonna get."

Mark led the way, sneaking downstairs. The continuous rain was keeping the adults indoors, and they could be heard laughing and talking from the living room.

They headed outside the back door, hovering in the porch to shelter from the rain.

"How are we getting there? We're not using the demon road." Mark warned.

Michelle held up some keys, giving them a shake. "We drive."

"Wait, are those Nanna's?" Mark froze. "We can't steal Nanna's car."

"We're borrowing it. We'll be back before anyone notices." Michelle countered. "Do you have any better suggestions?"

Mark wavered, torn behind his desire to meet these dark witches; and the risk that he would be grounded for eternity if his family found out.

"C'mon, it'll be a couple of hours' round trip." Michelle pushed, sensing him weakening. "They're all so distracted by the party and Nanna's new boyfriend, they won't know we're gone."

Mark felt he was going to regret it, "You can drive?"

"Duh, of course." Michelle shrugged. "I'd say I'm a better driver than Nanna anyways."

Mark snorted; they'd all been at the mercy of Nanna's chaotic driving.

He turned to Damian, who hovered silently at his side, a look of concern on his face.

"I'll... stay upstairs and cover for you. Then go with Aunt Maggie and Miriam when they head off." Damian said, his gaze dropping. His fingers hooked around Mark's hand possessively. "Stay safe."

Mark glanced over at Michelle. "Maybe you should go get the car started."

He waited for the goth girl to run through the rain, then turned back to his boyfriend. He traced his fingers across the tense line of Damian's jaw, watching his boyfriend visibly relax at his touch.

"I'll call you when we're on the way back." Mark promised quietly, as he leant closer.

Their lips met with a gentleness that soon faded into something more passionate. Mark pushed Damian against the wooden side of the porch, and he felt Damian's hands tangle into his hair, pulling Mark in for more.

Reluctantly, Mark paused, breathing hard against Damian's shoulder. 'I love you…' the words died on his lips. He'd already said it once without a similar reply from Damian; Mark didn't want to put his heart out there again.

Damian gave a crooked smile. "That was…"

"Yeah… I… best get going." Mark pulled away, and stepped into the rain.

Chapter Nine

Mark jogged over to the idling car, the warm rain helping to wash away the fuzziness of that kiss.

As soon as he got in, Michelle drove away with practised ease.

"So, who taught you to drive?" Mark asked conversationally. They were all a few months short of being seventeen and taking official lessons; he was impressed that Michelle had jumped the gun.

"A friend." Michelle said bitterly.

Mark tried again when the uncomfortable silence stretched on too long. "Is it true you stole a police car?"

"Ah, technically I didn't *steal* it, as I never left their premises." Michelle corrected. "I stayed in the police car park, trying to do a doughnut. I skidded into the chief's Rover, and it went downhill from there."

"Huh." Mark sat back, watching the countryside go past. None of his friends had ever done something so insane; stealing cars was a completely alien concept to him.

"Besides, didn't you steal a tractor recently?" Michelle asked.

Ah, Mark had forgotten about that. Perhaps it wasn't a totally alien concept. "*Borrowed*. And those were completely different circumstances."

"Yeah, tell me about it." Michelle snorted. "Everyone swoons when you nick a tractor to rescue your fella, and they scowl at me when I pinch a cop car."

"Yeah, people are weird like that." Mark muttered.

Even if they all thought he was heroic over Christmas, it hadn't taken much for the mob mentality of the school to turn against him. Mark didn't want to be cast as the villain again.

He glanced over to Michelle; she seemed to revel in being seen as someone dangerous. But Mark was fairly convinced that, even when she was juiced up on dark magic, Michelle would never have hurt any of them.

"Does this mean I'm a bad-ass like you, now?" Mark joked.

"Ha, you wish." Michelle snorted, casting a brief look at him. "Maybe you're a little less lame."

Mark grinned at the less-than-glowing compliment. "Too bad your dark witches don't have a Facebook group, then we could just contact them online."

"They do."

Mark blinked with surprise, "Really? I was only joking."

"What, you think dark magic worshippers and Facebook are incompatible?" Michelle shrugged, "It doesn't matter, though. We're not gonna get them to spill all their secrets over the internet. We need to see them in person."

Another uneasy silence filled the car as they trundled through dark countryside. When it got too much, Mark mentally flicked through potential conversations. He was about to speak, when Michelle raised a hand to stop him.

"If you even *think* of mentioning the demon realm *again*... I will slap you so hard, I'll lose control of the car and crash. That is how little I want to hear about it." Michelle snapped.

Mark bit his lip, sitting back in his seat. Maybe he had been going on about it a lot lately. "Noted."

The drive went smoothly enough. Mark didn't want to admit that Michelle had been right – she was a good driver. That still didn't stop Mark from gripping the arm rest more tightly, once they reached the motorway.

Eventually, the sprawling city of Sheffield lay before them.

Michelle drove past the colourful shopping centres, into the greyer part of town. Silent warehouses, and building blocks with black windows loomed on either side of the narrowing roads.

"Whatever you do, don't mention you've been to the demon realm." Michelle warned. "You'll become a demi-god in their eyes, and we'll never get them to focus on the info we want."

"Understood, I'll let you do the talking."

Michelle turned into a dark car park, and pulled up next to some battered-looking cars. Mark followed her lead, and got out, hunching against the rain. There was a pagan symbol etched above some rusted metal doors. Mark flinched as they stepped through, half anticipating the same magical barrier there'd been with the London coven; but there was nothing. Mark pulled on his magic, to confirm he could still access it, and breathed a sigh of relief. The symbol was just a symbol, there was no power behind it.

Music echoed from deep within, the bass making the floor tremble in time to the beat. Stepping into a large room, there was the smell of alcohol and incense. There was an eclectic collection of benches and chairs, strewn across the room.

There must have been a dozen people, all dressed in various shades of grey and black. They looked relaxed, a group of friends socialising, like any other. These just happened to be witches.

"Long time no see." A voice came from the shadows to their right.

Michelle raised her chin haughtily as a man stepped forwards. He looked to be a few years older than them, his brown hair was mousy and he had uneven stubble on his jaw.

"I've been busy, Joe. Exams coming up and all that." Michelle said dismissively.

The man's eyes turned to Mark, roving over him in open assessment. "Who's this?"

Mark could sense the man's aura tainted a sickly green with jealousy. Joe puffed out his chest, and pulled a weak layer of magic around him. Michelle had been right, without the aid of a demon, these dark witches weren't strong at all.

"This is Steve. He's one of Robert's recruits." Michelle said, the lie flowing easily.

Joe gave a half shrug, trying to not look like he cared about her response. "Want some?" He grunted, holding out a sweet-smelling roll-up.

Mark tried not to balk, he'd come across weed at parties before, but had never used it. He'd never even held it before, and was sure the dark witches would be able to tell.

Michelle snatched the joint out of Joe's hand. "He's not earnt it yet." She said with a cruel smile, taking a deep drag.

Joe seemed satisfied with her answer. "How'd it go in London? Did you get your answers?"

A flash of hurt crossed Michelle's face, before she hid it behind nonchalance. "I got the big answers. Robert came through on his promises."

"Do you guys want a drink?" Joe asked, looking solely at Michelle.

"Sure." Mark interjected, already fed up with being the third wheel. He could see why Michelle got extra-scowly around happy couples.

Mark had no intention of actually *drinking* what the dark witch gave him – he was still suspicious after Damian's old London neighbours had tried to drug him – but he figured he'd be accepted faster with a drink in hand.

Joe ran off to get drinks, leaving the two of them alone. Mark gave a questioning look at the joint that Michelle rolled in her fingers.

"It's only weed, stop with the judgmental looks." She snapped.

Mark chewed his lip, not sure what to say. He had embarrassingly little experience with drugs and real life; but he wondered what Nanna would say if she knew.

Michelle waved her hand at the other witches. "Weed helps take the edge off, when you're having dark magic withdrawals. Robert's visits here are sporadic – I don't think he cares what effect he has on the coven."

"What's that about Robert?" Joe piped up, returning with some warm beers.

"Just warning *Steve* that Robert is a law unto himself. There's no guarantee he'll see a demon tonight, just because it's Beltane." Michelle interjected.

Mark was impressed by how easily she seemed to weave her story. With Michelle and Harry's skilful lying,

Mark feared he'd never believe anyone again. Mark realised the other two were silent and waiting for his input.

"Bummer."

His weak response earned him an eyeroll from Michelle.

"Do y'know when Robert will be here?" Mark blurted out, then worried he was sounding too keen. "He gave me a taste of dark magic... I've never felt anything like it."

Joe looked smug at Mark's reaction, clearly thinking he was just another fanboy. "Demons work to their schedule, not ours. Sometimes Robert rocks up unannounced, otherwise he messages me when he wants the coven's aid."

Mark snorted. "How can you guys possibly help a demon? I mean... I can't imagine they'd ever need it, Robert being so powerful and all that." Mark bit his lip, stopping himself from rambling. He'd got the bumbling, ignorant idiot act down.

"There are lots of ways we help him; we're a vital part of his team." Joe nodded towards Michelle. "Or you can take Michelle's route, follow him around like a puppy and snog the face off him..."

Mark winced at the mental image of Michelle kissing his boyfriend. The sooner they got rid of Robert, the sooner Mark could go back to having Damian all to himself.

"Jealousy doesn't suit you." Michelle remarked, making Joe flush red.

There was an awkward silence, between one song ending, and another blasting out of the speakers.

Joe opened his mouth, but no sound came out.

"C'mon, I'll introduce you to the others." Michelle said, grabbing Mark's arm and dragging him further into the room.

Mark was surprised to find the group was pretty chilled, and not much different from the student parties he'd gone to. Not exactly what he thought demon minions would be like.

The dark witches laughed and chatted about the normal aspects of their lives, rarely commenting on magic or demons. It was hard to believe they were anything like Edith's evil coven.

They didn't share any information on their dealing with the demons, but Mark got the feeling that – except for perhaps their leader Joe – the dark witches didn't have any secrets to keep.

After an hour or so, Mark motioned to Michelle that they should leave. It would take some time to get home, and he could only pray no one had noticed their absence.

They ran through the rain, back to the car.

"Well, that was a waste." Mark stated.

Michelle started the car and headed back for the motorway. "I wouldn't say that." She pulled an unfamiliar mobile out of her pocket, and threw it into Mark's lap.

"What's this?"

"Joe's phone. He said Robert contacts him by text, we might find something of value."

Mark brought the screen to life, and frowned. "It's locked, genius."

"Really? Y'don't say." Michelle said. She was facing the road, but Mark was convinced she was rolling her eyes. "M."

"What?"

"The password. Draw the dots to make an 'M'."

Mark followed her instructions, and the phone magically unlocked. He looked to Michelle in query.

"It's just a crush on his part. Nothing ever happened between us."

Mark opened Joe's texts and scrolled through them. It didn't take long to find Robert's messages. It was highlighted as a favourite, even though there weren't many texts. Robert was direct and to the point, Joe's replies were hilariously long-winded and scrabbling for attention. Mark snorted at the desperation of the dark witch.

"Owt interesting?" Michelle asked.

"No, the last time he got invited to something was in February." Mark raised a brow. "Remember when your buddies trapped me in an underground tomb?"

Michelle grunted. "That was an extreme night."

Mark had to agree. The clash between Silvaticus and Robert was something he'd never forget. The stone monster against Robert's demon flame. The dark witches encircling them all, adding fuel to the fight.

"At least we'll be the first to know of any new plots." Mark tucked the phone into his pocket.

Chapter Ten

By Friday, everyone was ready to put aside the exam pressure, and enjoy Dean's party.

The rumour mill was working overboard, as usual. Supposedly, Dean was bringing a back-up dancer from Strictly as his date.

Everyone swore that he'd hired a miniature fairground to set up in his massive garden. And everyone was debating what music would be on. Dean had hinted that there'd be a live performance, and the students enjoyed arguing over who the performer would be.

Mark noticed that Harry got steadily paler throughout the day. He was so ashen-faced he looked like he was going to stack it.

"You OK?" Mark asked quietly.

"I dunno why I let you talk me into this; I can't do it. I'll give Dean his money back." Harry muttered.

"You can do it." Mark argued. "You've performed in front of much larger crowds."

"Yeah, but that's different." Harry protested. "I didn't know anyone, and I was on a stage. Tonight, they'll be *right there,* and I'll 'ave to see them all on Monday. What if they just laugh at me?"

Mark snorted, it was funny that the class clown was afraid of people laughing. "They won't." Mark insisted, then shrugged. "Worst case scenario – if it all goes tits up, we'll use a memory spell – no one will remember a thing."

Harry blinked at him. "Can you do that?"

"Sure."

"Huh."

Mark's attention was stolen by Damian. His boyfriend tore away from the other footballers as soon as he saw them, and made his way to Mark's side.

Damian's shirt sleeves were rolled up, managing to look ridiculously fashionable in their crappy school uniform. He dropped down, sitting on the grass next to Mark, and playfully nudged his boyfriend's shoulder.

"Hey, I have a question for you. I'll understand if you want to say no."

"What?" Mark prompted, not sure where this was going.

"Will you be my date tonight?" Damian asked, grinning.

"Cute, very cute." Mark snorted. "I'll think about it."

Damian looked happy with Mark's response, his blue eyes bright with amusement. When he bit his lip, that was all Mark could focus on…

"Ugh, if you two are about to start snogging, please can you warn me?" Harry moaned. "I can't stand other people's PDAs up close."

"Just your own." Mark countered, thinking the many times Harry and Sarah had been very public in their affection.

Damian rested his hand on Mark's, their fingers interlocking. He glanced up at Harry. "Fine, we promise. No snogging until tonight."

"None?" Mark asked, thinking there were a lot of hours between now and Dean's party.

"No public snogging." Damian amended.

*****

Mark and Damian kept their word, for the rest of the school day, although they did exchange some knowing looks.

The teachers had obviously gotten wind of the party, and knew that maintaining the attention of the GCSE students was impossible. They spent their time recapping old work, and didn't even try and get the pupils to be engaged.

That evening, his Dad gave Mark and Michelle a lift to the party, picking Damian up on the way. Mark was tempted to comment that this was the weirdest punishment he'd ever heard of, but he didn't want to remind his Dad that he'd been promised a lifetime of being grounded.

When they pulled up to Dean's house, the summer sun still shining brightly. Everyone was milling about the house, some dressed casually, others taking the rare opportunity to dress up.

Mark had gone for the standard jeans and shirt look, that hadn't let him down so far. Damian looked amazing in grey tailored shorts and red t-shirt that showed off his footballer's physique.

The others got out of the car, but Mark noticed that his Dad was grinding his teeth, looking worried.

Mark sighed, he missed the easy rapport he used to share with his father. He couldn't remember the last time that his Dad joked around.

"Mark, I know it might cramp your style…" His Dad began.

Mark snorted, fairly sure he had no style.

"But I want you to keep an eye on Michelle." Dad finished. "Nanna's worried about her; to be honest, I think we all want to see her stay safe."

Mark nodded. "I know, I will." He'd gotten used to his dark little shadow, and he had to admit that he cared about Michelle's safety, too.

"Alright." Dad said, with a forced smile. "And... promise, no dark magic tonight?"

"I promise." Mark replied. He still regretted using dark magic at Dean's last party, and he had the feeling his Dad was never going to let him live it down.

Mark watched the car disappear down the drive, before he turned to the house.

Harry and Sarah came out, looking very much the loved-up couple; and when Mark stood next to Damian, it left Michelle as the gooseberry.

"You can hang with us, if you want."

"Yeah, right." Michelle snorted, she went to duck inside to find her friends, but paused, looking uncertainly towards Harry. "Um, good luck tonight."

Michelle vanished indoors, leaving Mark's friends looking surprised.

"Wow, she's like, almost human now." Sarah remarked positively. "Your Nanna has worked miracles."

"Don't let Michelle hear you say that, she'll spit in your pop to rebalance the universe." Mark replied, sliding his hand into Damian's. "Let's go."

The party went as all parties before it. Despite the rumours, no one famous turned up as Dean's date; and only a sound system provided recorded tracks. The students drank, and danced, and all got more relaxed as the evening went on.

All except Harry.

Mark nudged his best friend, making sure he was still breathing.

Harry jumped at the contact, looking ghostly white.

"You can do this." Mark said for the umpteenth time. "You are amazing, and everyone is going to love you, you won't even need that memory spell."

Harry nodded, and with shaking hands, he went to get his guitar.

"Ladies and gentlemen!" Dean trilled from the makeshift performance area. He positively glowed as all attention focussed on him. "I promised live music, and here he is, the internet sensation; the next Ed Sheeran…"

"Ger'on wi' it!" Someone shouted during the dramatic pause, making the rest of the crowd laugh.

"Not-Dave!" Dean announced, with an extravagant flourish.

Dean jumped down, and was replaced by a much quieter Harry.

"That's not... Not-Dave."

"That's Harry..."

"Stop pratting around, mate."

Mark held his breath as the students around him playfully called out. Thankfully, none of them were jeering or being negative, but Harry's hands still shook as he pulled his guitar into place.

The first few chords were lost amongst the laughter, but all the chattering died down when he started to sing.

Relief flooded through Mark, he knew that his friend would be alright.

"Ouch." Damian whispered in his ear.

Mark blushed, not even noticing that he'd been holding Damian's arm in a vice-like grip. "Sorry."

With his limb free, he put his arm around Mark's waist. "He's really good."

Mark remembered that his boyfriend had only seen a video of Harry performing before, and this was his first time having the full experience. "Yes, he is." Mark replied, bursting with pride.

Chapter Eleven

Harry performed for nearly an hour, only pausing to sip at some water, and glance sheepishly towards his friends. Harry was enjoying himself, now that his nerves had burnt away.

When he finished his final song, there was whistling and clapping from his captive audience, and they bayed for more. The partygoers swarmed round Harry, suddenly seeing him as something more exciting than the fellow student he'd been just a few hours earlier. Somehow, Dean had managed to wriggle his way into the middle of the group, and was regaling them all with how he'd found out about Harry's singing talent.

Sarah jumped up from her perch. "I best go remind those girls – Harry already has a girlfriend."

She made her way over to the group, and Mark could see that some of the girls were indeed swooning over Harry and his guitar.

Damian chuckled, leaning into Mark. "Poor Sarah."

"Are you kidding?" Mark grinned. "Poor girls. Come on, I need a drink."

He laced his fingers with Damian's, and they headed to the kitchen, where Mark topped up their Coke. Damian grabbed some crisps, and they headed to a quieter part of the house.

Or, relatively quieter. The whole house seemed to be buzzing with the news that Harry – *their Harry* – had performed and was amazing. A group of students had found his Not-Dave Instagram account, and were discussing if that meant he was famous. One even announced they should get his autograph, before he gets *too* famous…

Mark was immensely proud of his best friend, and was glad that things had turned out so positively. Harry deserved it; he was one of the best people in the world.

Damian sat next to Mark on the small sofa. He turned so he was pressed up close to Mark; they'd never been this close in public, only when they were making out alone. Damian's hand idly traced up Mark's thigh, jolting Mark from his reverie.

"Penny for your thoughts?" He breathed into Mark's ear.

Mark met Damian's eye, wondering where this sudden public intimacy had come from. When he saw the black gaze, it all clicked.

"Robert? Seriously?" Mark shoved his hand away, and tried to bolt up from the seat.

Robert easily pushed him down onto the sofa, a crooked smile touching his lips. "Now, now, that won't do. What would your friends think if they saw you pushing away your boyfriend? Lovers' tiff perhaps?"

Robert's hands moved over Mark's thigh, a tingle of dark energy licking out across his skin.

Mark bit back a sigh, embarrassed that it should feel good. He reminded himself that this was Robert, the horny demon that had seduced Michelle, and had been trying to seduce him for months. "They'd find it just as out of character for Damian to be acting like a sex-mad demon. It's not his style." Mark said through gritted teeth.

"Fair point. I sometimes forget how dull my host is." Robert withdrew his hand slowly, but stayed uncomfortably close to Mark.

"Why are you here? Y'know, other than to ruin my life?" Mark asked.

"I came to find out how you are getting on with… your little mission."

"Already done." Mark replied quickly. "I went with Silvaticus to Brimcliff prison, and they agreed to call off the hell beasts."

"Impressive."

"I had a good motivation. Now, we're even. You're free to go, find a different host, maybe a willing one."

"Did you forget about our little chat? Your boyfriend is getting stronger by the day, do you think he'll want to go back to being a dull human again?" Robert's black eyes gleamed with amusement.

"You don't know Damian." Mark argued, he couldn't imagine his modest boyfriend being seduced by something like that.

"Really? You don't think it's crossed his mind to make the relationship more even?" Robert asked quietly. "He already thought he didn't deserve you when you first met; now you're becoming this powerful witch, how ever will he measure up?"

"Th-that doesn't matter to me." Mark said, but his heart dropped. Was it a concern to Damian?

"Your face has that serious look again." Robert commented, narrowing his eyes. "I'll leave you to mull things over. I need something better than this pop you keep foisting onto me."

Robert untangled his limbs from Mark and made his way back to the kitchen, cup in hand.

"Robert. You can't just..." Mark got to his feet, feeling uncertain. Damn that demon.

Mark followed the red shirt as it disappeared deeper into the house. He stopped in his tracks when he heard a crash. Ready for whatever unearthly threat was about to attack, Mark turned to see... Dean sitting on the floor, debris from smashed glasses and bowls all around him.

Mark weighed up his options and sighed. Robert seemed to be behaving himself so far, Mark could stop to help his classmate. He sighed, and gave Dean a hand.

Dean wobbled as he got pulled to his feet, and clung to the table for balance.

"I'll clean the worst up." Mark said, digging in the cupboards for a brush, to sweep up at least some of the glass.

"Well, if it isn't Witchy McWitchface!" Dean crooned, waving his arms wildly.

Mark rolled his eyes. Dean was clearly drunk. Again. "Harry's set went down real good." He said, trying to make polite conversation, as he dumped the shards of glass and pot in the bin.

"Shh." Dean grabbed Mark's arm, as he put a finger on his lips in a dramatic expression. Dean continued with a loud stage-whisper. "D'you think they all realise that Not-Dave is not... Dave..."

He giggled at his own joke.

"You're drunk." Mark stated, as Dean leant his unsteady weight against him. Mark could smell the sweet wine that lingered on his breath.

"Duh, it's a par-tay." Dean announced.

Dean went to walk back into the main room, but as soon as he left Mark's support, he stumbled.

"Ugh, dun feel good." Dean grumbled.

Mark knelt beside him and could see the tell-tale shivers and sheen of cold sweat on Dean's brow. It seemed a sorry part of growing up, that everyone experimented and drank to excess at least once. Mark had gotten drunk at one of Dean's parties last year, and it still made him flush with embarrassment that he'd hurled over the flowerbeds and felt awful for days.

"C'mon, let's get you t'bathroom." Mark said, gently lifting Dean from his crouched position.

"Told you – dun be nice." Dean moaned, staggering along with him.

They made it to the nearest bathroom, which was mercifully empty, and Dean dropped down next to the loo.

Mark closed the door, shutting out the music and noise of the other students partying. They didn't need to see Dean at his lowest.

As his not-friend threw up, Mark opened the window and waited. He idly rubbed Dean's back, thinking it might give some comfort.

"You shouldn' be 'ere." Dean groaned.

"Yeah, not really how I planned my evening." Mark confirmed.

"Dun wan' you 'ere. You... you..." Dean gave a shuddering sigh, "You dun wan' me."

"Seriously?" Mark groaned. "I thought we'd been over this – I don't dislike you."

"But you dun *like* me. Like... I like you. It's all crap."

Mark's stomach dropped. "What?"

Dean brushed his sweaty hair back, revealing his blood-shot eyes and dilated pupils. "I've always liked you. Everyone thought we'd make a cute couple; I was willing to wait for you to see sense. Then last year, at my party – you kissed me."

"What?" Mark thought back to the night he'd been an inebriated mess. "Uh, I was drunk, and we were playing spin the bottle. It wasn't real."

"It was for me." Dean said, resting his head against the cool side of the tub. "Afterwards, I got bored of waiting for you to act, so I arranged another party, get you to loosen up again, and… you bring Mr Perfect-Hair as your date."

"Dean, I-"

"Then you broke up, and I thought we'd finally have a chance, but you ended up with that Eric guy."

"Eadric." Mark corrected automatically, feeling a punch to the stomach at the mere mention of his late friend.

"I know." Dean gave a little shrug. "It's never me, it will never be me. You and Damian are the perfect couple, looking so loved up, it's sickening…"

"Dean-"

The bathroom door flew open, and Robert appeared in the doorway. "So this is where you're hiding… I thought I had you all to myself this evening."

"Robert, not now." Mark snapped. "If you're gonna be here, make yourself useful. Help me get Dean to bed."

Mark groaned at his own choice of words and didn't need to look at Robert, to see the innuendoes brewing. "Fine, I'll do it myself."

"You need to loosen up and live a bit." Robert said.

The demon moved to the barely-conscious Dean, and scooped him up with ease.

Mark blinked with surprise that he was actually being helpful, and wondered what the catch would be. "I'm not going back into your debt."

"I'm carrying a drunken boy to his room, it's hardly taxing; and not worth the creation of a deal." Robert replied dismissively.

Mark led upstairs, and checked each room until he found Dean's bedroom. It was mercifully empty. The room was decorated with white and silver, and had the same cold, minimalist feeling as the rest of Dean's expensive house. It looked flashy, but Mark couldn't imagine living in a place like this.

Robert put Dean on the bed with surprising care. The boy curled into his white sheets, snoring lightly.

"Thank you." Mark said.

Robert moved close enough to touch Mark's arm, the crackle of dark energy leaping between them. "If you really want to thank me..."

Mark snatched his arm back, instinctively. "You're wasting your time. I'm in love with Damian, it's always going to be him. I wouldn't expect a demon to understand."

"And pray, what do you know of demon emotions?" Robert said, unusually sombre. "I've been around for two thousand years; I've been in love a few times. I think I know more than you, witch."

"Really? Sorry, I just assumed..." Mark bit his lip. "I'm sorry."

"Humans always think love is going to last forever. Is Damian 'The One'?" Robert asked.

"Yes."

"The one you're going to marry? Have kids? Grow old together?"

"What?" Mark faltered, he hadn't thought about any of that. "We're only sixteen."

"Exactly." Robert smiled knowingly. "He's the one right now. There's no guarantee that he'll be the same man in five years, ten, fifty. You humans are so changeable in your short lives."

Mark wanted to argue back, but the words froze in his throat. "I love him."

"I know you do. For now." Robert said, with a shrug.

Chapter Twelve

The next day, Mark went to support the school football team, in what would be their last match before they broke up for summer. With the help of their new star striker, Damian, Tealford were no longer at their customary position at the bottom of the table. They were nowhere near the top, but it was the best they had finished in years, and everyone was excited.

The sun was warm, and the rain stayed away, so there were record numbers crowding the grounds to cheer on the team. Family, friends and schoolmates all hovered at the edge of the usually-rough pitch, which had been mown and repainted for the occasion.

Mark was standing with Harry and Sarah, who looked like they were still on yesterday's adrenaline rush. Michelle hovered at their side, not sure if she was officially part of the group.

The other teenagers kept shooting them knowing looks, now that they were in on the 'Not-Dave secret'. They kept playing with their phones, and Mark thought he heard little clips of Harry's singing.

Mark's parents were next to Damian's Aunt Maggie and her girlfriend Miriam. It seemed part of being an adult, was that you naturally gravitated towards the other adults. Mark guessed they all spoke the same language.

They cheered and whistled as the teams jogged out of the changing rooms, and up into the limelight. Damian winked as he passed them, before taking his place in the centre of the pitch.

Mark smiled, but it felt forced. The official whistle blew to start the game, and Mark watched Damian steal the ball, and drive it down the long pitch.

Damian had always been fast and agile, he looked confident and in control of the ball, shifting it seamlessly out of the path of opposing players. Mark had always loved to see Damian in what seemed to be his natural environment, but after his conversation with Robert, little doubts started to niggle. Did Damian look stronger, or was it just his imagination? It could have a mundane answer – Damian trained nearly daily with the football team, it was inevitable he would become stronger and better. Damn Robert for putting these thoughts in Mark's head.

Mark thought he heard his name, and snapped out of his reverie. "What?"

"I said you need to stop smiling, you look like a serial killer." Harry repeated.

"Sorry." Mark sighed. "Just thinking about what Robert said last night-"

"Robert? You spoke to Robert? When?"

"After you finished your set. He dropped in to check how things went in the demon realm."

Sarah shuddered, "I still can't believe you went to the *demon realm*. It's insane."

"No, what's insane is just casually dropping that you spoke to Robert last night. Why didn't you call for back-up?" Harry demanded.

"You were busy with your new fans." Mark shrugged. "Besides, Robert was on his best behaviour. Nothing happened."

"Absolutely nothing?" Michelle said bitterly. "He was practically dry-humping you at the party last night."

"I... didn't know you saw that." Mark blushed.

Harry looked in pain as he scrunched his eyes up, and pinched his nose. "Do we have to have this conversation *again*? Demons are *bad*. There is no 'best behaviour'. Promise me you'll call us when he next appears."

"I'm sorry, I promise." Mark mumbled. "All he did was help me put Dean to bed after he'd had too much to drink..."

He broke off as Damian took his first shot on goal. The Tealford supporters went mad when the ball flew past the dazed-looking goalie. Mark cheered and applauded, so proud of his boyfriend.

Damian looked embarrassed by the attention, and he glanced sheepishly towards Mark and his friends, before returning to the game.

The game restarted, with the opposition in possession, and the ball moved about midfield.

"Did, uh…?" Mark coughed, wondering how to phrase it. "It turns out Dean has a, um, crush on me."

"Well, duh." Harry said with a grin.

"What? You knew?" Mark felt a hot blush creep up his neck.

"It's like the worst kept secret in school, everybody knows." Harry confirmed. "Why do you think I always teased you about getting together with him?"

"But…"

"For a supposedly intuitive witch, you've been pretty obtuse on this. I've known for ages…"

"Ever since Sarah clued him in." Sarah added, jabbing her boyfriend's side.

Harry rubbed his ribs. "Ever since Sarah clued me in."

"Poor you, having another guy positively drooling over you." Michelle huffed. "I really don't get the appeal."

"Thanks." Mark replied, he could always rely on Michelle to bring his ego crashing back down.

Mark didn't know what to think. He'd assumed it was just the school rumour-mill that enjoyed the idea of him and Dean as a couple. He'd never thought there was any truth to it. Dean treated Mark with the same disdain as the rest of the pupils. "I think I'm gonna stick with Damian."

Harry snorted. "Good, can you imagine adding Dean to our circle? He's a walking migraine."

"Don't be mean." Sarah gave her boyfriend another less-than-subtle punch. "Although he does have a point, Damian is such a nice guy, and so handsome…"

Mark smirked that Sarah was still drooling over the relative newcomer. He couldn't blame her. He watched Damian run down the pitch, looking the perfect athlete.

"I can just imagine the buzz our boyfriends are going to make when we get back to school. Star singer and star striker." Sarah smiled. "You'll have to fight back his fans. Let me know if you need any help."

Mark followed Sarah's gaze towards a pack of girls that were shooting glances in Harry's direction.

"Thanks, but I think I should cope. I don't have any other gay guys to contend with." Mark replied, in what he hoped was an airy manner. The only other student who was out, was Dean; and except for a few choice remarks, he'd shown no interest in chasing Damian. The fact that Dean was interested in Mark was a fact that he was struggling to get his head around.

*****

The rest of the weekend passed without any further excitement. Monday morning brought with it the added stress of The First Exam.

Strangely, most of the Year 11 students seemed in a good mood, thanks mainly to Dean's party. It was the first time they had all been together again since Harry's performance, and many of the students had smug smiles, being in on the 'Not-Dave' secret.

Dean looked like he was enjoying lording over the masses, being the one that had brought Not-Dave to their attention. He lapped up the praise from everyone, but after his drunken confessions that night, he sheepishly avoided Mark and his friends.

The teachers looked puzzled by the upbeat atmosphere, as the pupils gathered by the main hall, waiting to file in for their exam.

Mark stood waiting with his friends. Damian was at his side, leaning against him. Mark noticed his boyfriend's nervous foot-tapping that vibrated through his whole body. He took Damian's hand and squeezed it reassuringly. Damian gave him a fleeting smile.

Sarah still clung to Harry's arm; in fact, Mark had not seen them separated since Harry's performance on Friday. Mark wondered if it was only pride, or a less-than-subtle reminder to Harry's new female fans that he was taken.

Several people came up to their group, to congratulate Harry with varying levels of awkwardness. Some shyly asked when his next gig was, and his manager smiled and told them about the show in Leeds next month.

When another pair of students walked away, Sarah's smile slipped. "I'm missing out on an opportunity. I should have flyers for the next performance, or at least business cards!"

"Stop being hard on yourself." Harry said, grabbing both of Sarah's hands in his, and pulling her close. "You have been an amazing manager, and I'm happy with how my career is progressing."

As his best friends got smoochy, Mark turned away. He saw Damian looking equally sheepish, being stuck close to their public display of affection.

"I can't believe I'm gonna say this, but I wish they'd get on with the exam." Mark said quietly, making his boyfriend chuckle.

As though tempting fate, their English teacher came to officially start the exam process.

The upbeat mood suddenly stilled, as everyone filed into the dining room, which had been converted into an exam hall. Rickety wooden tables formed strict rows across the floor. Mark headed to his assigned seat, and made himself as comfortable as possible on the plastic chair with bent legs.

Their English teacher, Mr Black, stood at the front, and once everyone was seated, he read through the exam procedure and rules.

Mark sighed, tuning out of the spiel. He felt queasy, remembering how they would have to sit through this at the start of every exam. As though his fellow students needed reminding that cheating wasn't allowed, and that you couldn't talk to others…

"…you have one and a half hours. Good luck." Mr Black finally finished.

Mark sighed, and opened his exam paper.

*****

After the exam, the unusually upbeat mood of the student populace had disappeared; replaced by relief that the first one was over; and self-flagellation at their answers.

Mark and his friends had long since agreed not to discuss their exams. There was no point going over answers that could not be changed. They now had an extra-long break for lunch, before their first Maths exam this afternoon.

After the miserably wet weekend, the weather was bright and sunny, with the promising warmth of summer. The sports field was already littered with groups of students, who were in that post-exam daze.

Mark and his friends found a vacant patch and made themselves comfortable.

Mark noticed Michelle and her posse passing by, probably going for a smoke in the old bike shed again. He nodded in greeting, and she nodded back.

"So, how's it going with Michelle?" Sarah asked, noticing where he was looking.

"OK, I guess. She has more good days than bad, now."

"If she's feeling better, d'you think she'll go home?"

Mark hesitated. He didn't like the thought of Michelle going back to her parents – they had ignored her very existence for months. "There's no rush."

"I saw her mum at the bank the other day, I mentioned that Michelle was getting on well, and there was zero reaction." Sarah sniffed. "I don't get how parents can be so blah. Maybe she can stay with you guys, your house is plenty big enough."

Mark hadn't shared the truth about Michelle's birth-mother being the evil dark witch Edith. Her whole family seemed screwed. Her *adopted* parents had actively chosen to take her on as a daughter; it just seemed cruel that they could be so dismissive of her now. Yes, Michelle lashed out, but Nanna had been right all along – there was a scared little girl beneath it all.

"I wouldn't be opposed to her being a more permanent addition." Mark said.

There was an uncomfortable silence, so Harry decided to fill it with a sharp slap on Mark's arm.

"Ow! Not necessary." Mark couldn't help but laugh at his best friend's random ways of expressing support.

"Are you coming to mine later to study?" Harry asked. "Mum's cooking."

"Sure, I'll bring the pizza." Mark replied, knowing the routine when Mrs Johnson dared to cook.

Chapter Thirteen

After the day of exams, Mark was relieved to head home. He had another exam in the morning. Sixteen hours and counting. The other GCSE students on the bus were dissecting their tests and various answers, bemoaning their results.

Mark was glad to get off at his stop, with Michelle on his heels.

The pleasant day was getting overcast, and a few icy drops had begun to fall by the time the house was in view. Summer storms weren't uncommon, but this one was rolling in with unusual speed. The clouds blackened and the wind picked up, as the first flash of lightning crackled along the sky.

Mark jogged through the rain, heading for shelter in Nanna's kitchen. The door was open and the room empty. The Aga was stone cold, and there was no sign of life.

"Nanna?" Mark called, shrugging off his wet coat.

"Your turn for making tea." Michelle insisted as she followed him into the kitchen.

Mark snorted. "It's *always* my turn."

"Yes." Michelle agreed. "That's how it works, isn't it?"

Mark grunted at her skewed humour, and headed into the living room. He found Tigger curled up in Nanna's favourite armchair, but still no sign of her.

"Do you think she's forgotten our lesson?" Michelle piped up. "Maybe she's off with her farrier boyfriend."

"The back door is open..." Mark hovered in the doorway, the large family garden stretched out before him.

Behind the grey sheet of rain, Mark thought he saw a figure.

"Nanna!" He called, a deep rumble of thunder drowning his voice.

Mark ran out into the garden, the rain quickly drenching his school jumper. He was vaguely aware of Michelle following him. The air was oppressive and Mark felt that something unnatural was driving the storm. In response to his fear, Luka appeared. Michelle's crow spirit flew haphazardly through the rain.

"Nanna!" Mark yelled.

They were close enough to see Nanna walking away from the house, ignorant of the rain that soaked them all. She half-turned at his voice, and hesitated.

"Michael?" Her voice trembled, hard to hear over the storm. Her eyes turned to Michelle. "Edith?"

They didn't have a chance to say anything, before there was a wave of magic that seemed to ripple through the ground. Nanna's magic was wild and suffocating.

Luka and the crow stood defensively between the teens and Nanna, their spirit magic working to nullify the spell.

"Nanna!" Mark cried. It felt like there was a barrier through which he couldn't push. She was still focussed on Michelle – if she was confusing her for Edith, it would explain the attack.

Mark didn't have time to wonder what could have occurred to affect Nanna, what spell could cause the hallucination; he realised he'd have more chance of calming the situation if Michelle wasn't there.

"Go back to the house." He ordered, then added. "Find my mum – she's a nurse..."

He waited for Michelle to disappear towards the house, another flash of lightning highlighting her path.

"Nanna!" Mark tried again.

Nanna looked at him with unseeing eyes. Her usually sharp thoughts were visibly sluggish. "Michael?"

The magic in the air lessened, and Mark felt like he could move closer.

"You don't do magic, Michael." Nanna said, a fearful tremor in her voice.

Mark decided there was no point arguing with Nanna, although it was disturbing that she thought he looked so much like his Dad. "Nanna, come back inside."

Mark got close enough to put his arm around her, to gently guide her to the house. Nanna's cardigan was soaked through, and Mark was shocked by how physically frail she felt against him.

Nanna relaxed into his arms, immediately dropping the spell she had been maintaining. Mark suspected she had initiated the storm, and even though she was no longer fuelling it, the weather continued. The rain still hammered down, and the threat of thunder rumbled overhead.

Mark walked slowly with Nanna back to the house, half scared that any sudden movements would set her off again.

Luka ran a few steps ahead. He kept stopping to watch them, his head cocked aside, for once uncertain of the danger his master was in.

Mark's Mum came running out of the house, her face dark with worry. "Did she hurt you?"

Mark shook his head. "We're all fine. Something's happened to Nanna. Maybe a curse, or poison?"

Mum pursed her lips, but didn't respond to him. "Nanna, it's Agatha. We'll go inside and get you into some dry clothes."

Nanna still looked confused, but allowed herself to be steered into her half of the house. Mark's Mum switched into full-nurse-mode. "Please check that Michelle's alright. She seemed distressed when she was running in."

Mark found Michelle sitting in Nanna's living room, with Tigger curled up in her lap. Her crow spirit was perched on the back of her chair, its wet feathers looking darker than ever.

Aware of how soaked everyone was, Mark started a fire with a simple spell. The fireplace soon became a decent blaze, and Luka curled up in front of it, like a normal dog.

"What happened out there?" Michelle asked, her voice hoarse.

"I've no idea." Mark replied weakly.

They sat in silence for an age, neither feeling like working on their spells or revision for tomorrow.

Eventually there were footsteps coming downstairs, and Mark's Mum and Nanna both made their way into the living room.

Mum settled Nanna into her favourite chair, then went to fetch a flask of her famous magic tea.

Mark watched them impatiently. "What happened?"

Nanna looked at Mum, her skin grey and tired. Mark had never seen her look so worn.

"Nanna was recently diagnosed with dementia." Mum said quietly.

"W-what?" Mark asked, completely lost.

"Um, maybe I should go." Michelle piped up.

"No, both of you stay." Mum said in her nurse's voice. "It's important that the people closest to Nanna know what's happening."

"What is dementia?"

"It's a disease that progressively destroys brain cells. It can lead to confusion, problems with memory, amongst other things." Mum squeezed Nanna's shoulder. "Nanna's in the early stages, but we think the symptoms may have been exasperated by the magic."

Mark sat numbly, it all sounded so serious and life-altering. It sounded like something that belonged to other families, other people.

"Can you fix it?" Michelle's voice trembled.

"It can be managed with meds and care, but it's irreversible." Mum said.

"What about healing with magic?" Mark asked.

His Mum hesitated, looking towards Nanna, as it wasn't her area of expertise.

"No." Nanna said, not meeting their eyes, her voice weak and broken. "Magic simply increases the body's natural healing process. What's happening to me... if magic mimics my brain cells, they may disintegrate faster."

Mark shivered. He'd never heard Nanna sound so downtrodden. Nanna seemed to realise it, too, and she forced some perkiness for the kids.

"My life isn't over, far from it. I won't let this disease stop me from having fun." Nanna snapped. Then she sighed, squeezing Mum's hand. "There may be a problem with my... control over magic. As you know, magic relies heavily on a witch's intention. I can't... it has been slipping out of hand for a while now."

Mark looked between his Mum and Nanna. Were there clues he had missed? "Is there anything I can do?"

His Mum and Nanna exchanged a weighted look, making him nervous.

"We've discussed your heritage..." Nanna began, slowly. "You're from a powerful bloodline, but the magic linked to the Grand High Witch is a completely different entity. It was always our plan to pass it on to you, Mark. Eventually, after you'd been to uni, had a life... but this *thing* means we have to speed up our timetable."

Nanna glanced at Mark's Mum. "I've discussed it at length with your parents, and we think the Summer Solstice will be the optimum time for the exchange. You'll have finished your exams, and still have a couple of months before college starts, which will give you time to... adapt."

Mark sat dazed, Nanna had been vaguely training him to take over her role, but he was far from ready. There was so much about magic that he didn't know. He'd never even met any of the other covens and witches, and now he was supposed to lead the community? "T-that's less than a month away."

Nanna nodded. "I know it's not ideal..."

Mark stood up, suddenly feeling overheated, packed into that little room surrounded by people. "I... I need to get out."

He pushed passed a startled-looking Michelle, and dashed outside, grabbing his cagoule as he went.

"Mark?"

Mark heard his Dad's voice from the other side of the house. Mark didn't want to talk to him right now; he didn't want to hear the logic behind his family planning his future for him. He ran through the rain to the garage and pulled out his bike.

The lightning storm had abated, and only a cold wind still stirred. Mark didn't know where he was heading, just that he wanted to be alone. Luckily in the countryside, he didn't have to go far, to feel like he was leaving the world behind.

*****

Mark sat behind a stone wall, the wet ground soaking through his jeans. At least the rain had stopped, although the dark clouds still threatened more.

Mark closed his eyes. As he breathed in, he felt the energy of the dissipating storm, like friction in the air; as he breathed out, he felt the earth beneath him like a slow, beating heart of power. Nature was all around him, and it was instinctual for his magic to merge with it.

Just like at Eadric's funeral, Mark felt calmed by being connected to something much bigger than himself.

It was hard to believe that two months had passed already. Sometimes, it felt like yesterday; other times, like it was a lifetime ago. Mark felt a spark of remorse that he wasn't crippled by grief anymore. Some days, he was guilty of not even thinking of his friend.

The peace was ruined by a loud, sputtering engine. Mark reluctantly opened his eyes to see a familiar blue dirt bike heading his way.

"Ay up."

Mark looked up at Harry's greeting. "Hey, what you doin' here?"

"When you stormed off in your dramatic storminess, your Mum decided to call in the big guns, to make sure you were alright." Harry said with a shrug.

Mark tried to smile, but it just turned into an awkward face movement. "I'm impressed you found me."

"Michelle did the same location spell you did in London. Except hers didn't blow up." Harry dropped down on the ground next to Mark, leaning against the stone wall.

The two boys sat in silence for a while. After all the years they had spent together, there seemed to be a new tension between them, which Mark found unsettling.

"I miss us." He murmured.

"I'm right 'ere, you numpty." Harry said, his joking falling a little flat.

"Y'know what I mean. I miss how easy things used to be." Mark tilted his head back, the rough stone digging into his skin, with a discomfort he could deal with.

"I miss it too." Harry confessed. "But things were always going to change, high school is ending."

"Yeah, it was all going too fast with girlfriends and boyfriends, and college coming up..." Mark sighed. "Now... it's dizzying. I've only just started magic training, and now they want me to jump straight to the end game. I don't even know what I want to do in my life, and now I don't have a choice."

"That's life, dude. Do you think everyone gets what they want?"

Mark looked over at Harry's less-than-comforting words. "Great pep talk."

"That's what I'm here for." Harry replied. "Look, you're not the only person in the world who has to step up earlier than planned to help their family. Sure, you're probably the only one I know with a magical reason..."

"It's not just that..." Mark said with a sigh. "How can I be the 'Grand High Witch'? I'm practically a novice. Danny's done nowt but belittle me since I met him, and I can imagine lots of other witches will think like him."

"Danny is an arrogant git. Ignore him."

"You've never met him." Mark said with a snort.

"Yeah, but I've heard you rant about him. It's my duty as your best friend to consider him a git."

"Appreciated." Mark said, honestly. He didn't know what he'd do without Harry.

"Ready to go back and apologise to your family for skipping out?" Harry asked, standing up and knocking the dirt off his jeans.

"Ugh, I deserve to burn in hell, don't I?" Mark picked idly at some grass by his foot. "Nanna's the one going through all this..."

"Well, you're all going through it; so maybe just a light roasting." Harry offered his hand. "Anyway, I thought you said the demon realm was all cold seas and cliffs?"

Mark let himself be pulled to his feet. "I only saw one part. I imagine the part Robert comes from is more fiery."

Chapter Fourteen

Mark didn't know how he got through the next week. He tried to focus on the exams, as much as the other pupils, but he found it impossible to concentrate for any period of time. His Nanna had always been this indestructible figure, who stepped in to rescue Mark every time he made a stupid mistake. From what his Mum had told him about the disease (and some late-night internet searches when he couldn't sleep), it would slowly steal away everything that made Nanna who she was *now*. One day, Mark may even become a stranger in her eyes, and that terrified him.

With the exception of his closest friends, the other students were ignorant of the thoughts that plagued Mark. The way they went about their lives, as though everything was perfectly normal... it jarred against Mark's new reality.

Despite how amazing Harry, Sarah and even Damian had been, with their unfailing sympathy; Mark found an unexpected support. Michelle was feeling pain almost as acutely as Mark did.

It shouldn't have been a surprise; the girl had lived with Nanna for months. Despite their early, violent clashes, Nanna was the closest thing to a *real* family-figure that Michelle ever had. When Mark saw Michelle's hesitant concern, it was a heart-breaking mirror to his own.

At home, his Mum and Dad seemed to be walking on eggshells, being very careful not to say anything that could upset the kids. It was kindly meant, but it made Mark feel even worse. It was a constant reminder that it was his parents who would have to take on the role of main carers one day, switching roles with their matriarch.

Nanna was the victim of something she couldn't control, but she quickly got tired of people treating her like she was fragile. She finally snapped and told them that they were stuck with her for many years to come; and the next person to treat her like she was on her deathbed would get a curse that would make locusts and boils look mild.

When Damian turned up on Saturday morning, breaking the tense atmosphere, Mark was relieved.

"Want to go for a ride?" Damian piped up, looking very pleased with himself.

Mark's family practically shoved him out of the door; he guessed his dark moods hadn't been helping matters. "Sure."

He grabbed his bike from the garage, then went to join his boyfriend.

"Nice bike." Mark commented, nodding at the very shiny, very new, red bike that Damian had hold of.

"Yeah, Aunt Maggie got it me." Damian replied, with a genuine smile. "It was supposed to be a post-exam present, but when it got delivered yesterday, she got too excited to wait any longer."

"It is looking very clean. Let's go christen it." Mark grinned. "Where do you wanna go, the village?"

"Leave it all to me. I have plans." Damian said mysteriously, kicking off and setting down the gravel driveway.

Mark hurried after him, but Damian refused to explain any further.

"Fine, keep yer secrets." Mark huffed as he caught up with his boyfriend. He matched Damian's pace, so they could ride together on the empty country roads. "How's things at home?"

"Alright. Miriam's all settled in now, it feels like she's been there forever." Damian smiled, already fond of his aunt's girlfriend. "Although the cottage is pretty cramped now, I think they're looking forward to when I bugger off to uni."

Damian's Aunt Maggie had bought the house when she was on her own. She never would have predicted that her sister would be killed in a car crash, and that her teenage nephew would move in; quickly followed by a live-in girlfriend after a whirlwind romance.

"Maybe Maggie and Miriam will buy a bigger place, now they're an official couple." Mark suggested.

Damian gave a half-hearted shrug. "Yeah, I kinda like the cottage, though. It feels like home."

"Have you told Maggie about you-know-who?" Mark asked, already guessing the answer.

Damian didn't reply, his attention fixed on an upcoming track. "Let's go off-road."

Mark didn't push the matter, he knew that Damian was still sensitive about sharing his body with a demon, and tended to ignore Robert's existence.

Mark followed as his boyfriend headed up a track that was half-stone and half-dried-mud. It made for harder work, and Mark stood up, pushing his weight onto his pedals.

Damian seemed to be coping better. Mark wondered if it was the new bike; the football training; or the extra demon-fuelled strength he'd been exhibiting lately.

"Come on, slow coach!" Damian teased.

Mark felt the sweat bead across his skin. The sun beat down with a real summer heat, and he wished he'd brought a drink with him. Mark focussed on keeping up, concentrating on Damian's back wheel, and coughing as dry dirt kicked into his face.

Soon enough, Damian stopped at the crest of a hill, waiting for Mark to join him.

Mark got his bearings, and suddenly felt uneasy. They were near the stone ruins that made up Eadric's grave. Mark hadn't been here since the funeral at Ostara, two whole months ago. After finally being absent from his daily life, Mark's grief hit as raw and real as those first days. The shock of it squeezed the breath out of his chest, and Mark tried to swallow down the lump of emotions that rose in his throat.

When he turned to his boyfriend, Damian was looking pale and worried. "Shit, I completely forgot... I'm sorry, Mark. I forgot this was here. It's... it's the only route I know."

Not trusting his voice, Mark nodded his acceptance of Damian's apology.

"Um, are you OK to carry on? We'll... keep our distance." Damian offered. "Unless, um... you want to go see him..."

Mark shook his head. He didn't want to go pay his respects to Eadric. It wouldn't change anything; it wouldn't bring Eadric back to life, and it wouldn't stop Mark from being guilty of leading him to his death.

Damian looked like he was sharing Mark's pain. He'd always been so sensitive and attuned to those around him, Mark didn't want Damian to blame himself for this dark spot, too.

"This isn't your fault. I can't go around avoiding everywhere that makes me think of Eadric. I have to move on with life, especially if I need to step up and help Nanna." Mark said, his voice shaking slightly.

His words were some relief to Damian, who turned his bike down the track. "I, um... you mentioned that we could go swimming in the river in summer. I thought it might be fun; but we can go back, if you'd rather-"

"No!" Mark interrupted, the image of Damian jumping in the river with nothing but his shorts on was very appealing. "I mean, we're already here, it'd be a waste of a nice day..."

Without waiting for Damian's response, Mark set off towards the best swimming spot, where the river was wide and deep, with few rocks in the way. It was protected by a grassy knoll, that kept the worst of the wind away, making the bank a positive sun trap.

"You should have told me, I didn't bring my swimming gear." Mark shouted over his shoulder, a smile creeping over his lips. "Unless you're suggesting skinny-dipping."

"No skinny-dipping." Came a familiar voice. "Nobody wants to see your pasty arse."

"Harry? What are you doing here?" Mark skidded to a stop, finding the best spot was already occupied by Harry, Sarah, and even Michelle.

There were rucksacks and towels scattered across the grassy bank. Harry was armed with a bottle of sun lotion, and half-way through coating Sarah's back.

"It was Damian's idea." Harry turned back to his girlfriend.

Mark's boyfriend looked sheepish at the subterfuge, but a little pleased with himself. "I thought you might need a distraction; preferably away from home, school, exams and demons."

Mark was choked up by everything. His boyfriend had to be one of the kindest and most considerate people on Earth; and he couldn't wish for better friends. "It's perfect." He said, squeezing Damian's hand.

"My mum packed us a picnic." Harry pulled a face at his mother's poor cooking. "But we can just chuck that in the bin."

"S'OK, Nanna made enough food for an army." Michelle opened her stuffed rucksack, and wrestled out a towel and some swimming trunks. She threw them at Mark. "I agree with Harry, no one wants to see your pasty arse."

They all got changed, and Mark ran and leapt into the deepest part of the river, knowing it was the best way to deal with the cold water. The breath rushed out of him, as an icy cold wrapped around his body. Mark tread water, and grinned up at Damian.

His boyfriend followed his example, and jumped in, a little more cautiously. He hit the water, and let out a scream, his face red. "It's friggin' freezing!"

Mark laughed at his expression. "What did you expect?"

"W-we used t-to go swimming at C-camber Sands. Very different." Damian said, his teeth chattering. "Ssandy beach, warm water. C-crowds of people, as far as the eye could see."

"Yeah, a little different." Mark agreed, looking at the coarse grass and empty moors.

They soon warmed up, racing each other down the river. The ever-competitive Sarah put the boys to shame, and won all her rounds. Until Harry declared that she must be cheating, and proceeded to dunk her.

When she came up spluttering, it all devolved into chaos. Water was splashed everywhere, and at everyone.

Laughing, Mark made his way out of the river, and grabbed a drink from Michelle's stash.

Michelle was sitting on her towel, still fully-clothed, reading a book. At her side, was her crow spirit; Michelle idly stroking its black feathers.

"Are you sure you don't want to come in the river?" Mark asked for the umpteenth time.

"Er, no." Michelle said, sneering at the immature play that was happening in the water.

"You can just do your own thing." Mark insisted.

"I am doing my own thing." Michelle snapped, waving her book in his face.

"No, I meant you can have a quiet swim on your own, they'll leave you in peace, if that's what you want." Mark gestured to the river. "There's no guarantee we'll have nice enough weather again this summer."

Michelle glared up at him, her eyes narrowed; but Mark thought he saw a flicker of something. Was she afraid? Was that why her crow spirit was keeping her company?

"Are you alright?"

"Fine." She snapped.

Mark rolled his eyes. "What did you tell me: no one believes that passive-aggressive response?"

"I... can't swim." Michelle said so quietly, Mark barely heard her.

"What?" Mark was surprised that this was the source of her fear today. "Sorry, I just assumed..."

"Yeah well, my parents never took me to lessons, or foreign holidays with seas to swim in." Michelle hissed.

Mark stood gormlessly, he'd had both in his past, and he'd taken for granted that he could swim. It seemed a basic skill, and had never thought that other people might not have the same training. "Oh. D'you... want to learn?"

Michelle looked over at Mark's friends with envious eyes, as they swam confidently through the river. "No." She replied.

Mark guessed she didn't want to show any weakness in front of the others, and he could understand that. "Another time, then."

Michelle stared at him for so long, that Mark thought he must have sprouted antlers.

"Right..." He muttered, breaking her gaze. He nodded to the crow. "I was surprised to see her out, there's nothing more dangerous than Mrs Johnson's picnic food."

"I figured she'd appreciate it." Michelle replied, seemingly happy with the change of topic. "It's pretty lousy, if all she ever sees is fighting."

"Oh." Mark had never thought what their protective spirits did when they weren't in physical form. Did they have a spirit world, where they led spirit lives? Or did they only exist when they were summoned?

Deciding it couldn't do any harm, Mark closed his eyes and focussed on Luka. He knew that he was successful, when he felt a warm weight lean against his bare leg. When he opened his eyes, the black and white border collie looked up at him with his focussed sheep-dog stare.

"Go… have fun." Mark made an awkward gesture to the river.

The spirit looked between the two groups and, sensing no danger, trotted towards the river.

"Luka!" Harry cried in delight.

Mark's best friend hadn't been allowed a family pet growing up, and he was easily Luka's biggest fan. The protective spirit fully-embraced being a dog, and barked at the playing teens, waggy its tail, before jumping into the water to join them.

Chapter Fifteen

They stayed at the riverside for hours. It was the perfect break from all the stress at school and home; Mark could have happily stayed longer, but the clouds started to roll in and the temperature was quick to drop on the sparse moors.

They eventually packed everything up, and picked up their bikes. Harry and Sarah headed due south, the straightest route home.

Mark and Damian faced West to go back to Damian's cottage for a movie night. There was an awkward moment where Damian invited Michelle, too.

The girl gazed at him longingly, for a little too long for comfort, before rejecting the offer. She made her way back to Nanna's house alone.

Trying not to feel too bad for the girl that kept making eyes at his boyfriend, Mark set off, knowing the way to Damian's house off by heart.

"So, Prom is less than two weeks away." Damian commented, as he rode up to Mark's side. "Have you got your suit sorted?"

"Why, are you asking me to be your Prom date?" Mark teased. To be honest, he'd totally forgotten about getting a suit. "I'll still be able to rent one, right?"

"In London's many stores – no problem." Damian frowned. "In Tealford's one store, when everyone needs a tux in the same week…?"

"Huh. Maybe I can still get one at York Outlet." Mark muttered. His only other option was borrowing a suit from his Dad; but he shuddered at the thought of turning up to Prom with a hot date, and an ill-fitting old-fashioned suit. "Want to go tomorrow?"

Damian didn't reply, his eyes were fixed on something ahead.

"Is that… smoke?" Mark gasped at the dark plume that was rising in the distance.

It was a long way from Bonfire Night, and Mark felt a stab of unease. The two of them started to pedal harder, kicking their speed up a notch.

The smoke was coming from Damian's village. As they got closer…

"Is that your cottage?" Mark saw thick smoke rising from the thatch roof. "Surely Miriam can handle it."

It was just fire, one of the elements that the witches trained with frequently. Mark guessed that his more experienced covenmate already had this under control.

Damian's Aunt Maggie was stood in the road, in front of the house. She was on her mobile to the emergency services, patches of black on her clothes, but otherwise unhurt.

She saw the boys arrive, and grabbed Damian in a one-armed hug. "It's safe, we're fine, it's all fine." She babbled.

"What happened?" Damian asked.

"W-we don't know, maybe an electrical fault? It just started to burn. Miriam's doing what she can to keep it under control." Maggie said, her voice shaking, as she resolutely kept her phone glued to her ear. Her eyes rested on Mark. "Can… you're a witch, too. Can you help her?"

Mark nodded. Miriam was more skilled than him, but Mark had to do what he could. He glanced over at Damian and his aunt. "Stay safe."

Mark jogged to the side of the cottage where Miriam stood with a fierce look of concentration, and arms raised.

"Hey, what do you need me to do?" Mark shouted over the crackling fire. This close to the house, the heat made him buckle.

Miriam frowned at the cottage, struggling to concentrate on her spell, and speak to Mark. "Feed your energy… into… mine. Or, um… summon rain…"

Mark wasn't confident in summoning rain, so he stood next to Miriam, and searched for her magic. She was pouring everything into a spell that should have stopped the fire already, Mark couldn't figure out why it wasn't working.

Mark closed his eyes and tried to find an inner peace, despite the chaos around him. He then channelled his magic into Miriam's spell. And… nothing happened. Despite the heat, Mark shivered as he watched their combined strength dissipate against the fire.

It wasn't natural.

Mark focussed on the fire, moving past the flames and heat, until he got to the core and confirmed his suspicions. Magic had started this fire. Mark felt the familiar, suffocating rhythm of demon magic. He'd been around it so much lately, it glowed like a beacon to his senses.

"Dark magic." Mark stated, pulling his senses back.

"What?" Miriam spat, scowling at the effort of maintaining her spell.

Mark's thoughts were spinning. They could only minimise the damage. It would take a witch of Nanna's strength to counter the demon magic… or a demon…

Mark jogged back to where Maggie and Damian stood frozen in helplessness by the roadside. Some of the neighbours had emerged from their houses, offering buckets, blankets, and hot drinks.

Mark grabbed his boyfriend's sleeve and pulled him away from his aunt. "I think we need Robert's help."

"What? Why?" Beneath his summer tan, Damian blanched. He looked about at the crowd. "I dunno if it's a good idea..."

"Whoever started this fire used dark magic. Only Robert can stop it." Mark said quietly, he took Damian's hand, lacing their fingers together. "It's the only way to save the cottage. Nanna could break the spell, but by the time she gets here…"

Damian looked at the house with a pained expression. It had been his home for six months, somewhere he'd finally started to be happy. "Fine."

Close to, Mark could see the black bleeding into Damian's blue eyes, until Robert stood before him. The demon increased his grip on Mark's hand, his thumb trailing suggestively over his wrist.

"No time for that." Mark said, snatching his hand away. "We need your help."

Robert turned his gaze to the house, the flames really starting to take hold on the thatch roof. His arrogant expression froze, as he took in the facts. "A demon started this fire."

"Yeah, I guessed as much." Mark muttered. "Can you help stop it?"

"Why would…" Robert's voice trailed off, and the demon nodded. Robert strode confidently towards the danger. He raised his arms, "*Geændung.*"

With a single word, he'd overcome the spell that had thwarted both Mark and Miriam's skills. Mark noticed that the fire was no longer fuelled by magic. It was already starting to recede, but Robert followed it up by another spell, completely extinguishing the blaze.

The fire had gone, but everything was still chaotic. No strangers to witches' magic, the neighbours cheered, and Mark could hear the sound of sirens in the distance. Perfect timing.

At his side, Robert was being unusually quiet. Mark had expected the demon to follow up his help with another inappropriate suggestion. Mark had to admit that a part of him was disappointed to only get silence.

"Do you think someone was trying to kill you?" Mark asked.

"I don't know whether you've noticed, but I'm a fire demon." Robert gave him a withering look. "I can't burn. If someone was trying to harm me, they'd be better using water, like that damned prison in Brimcliff."

At the mention of the prison, a cold shiver ran up his spine. Mark could imagine that for a creature of fire, that cold damp place was an extra level of torture.

"No, I think someone was trying to frame me." Robert finished.

Mark looked at him in surprise, "Why?"

"For some nefarious reason, I have no doubt." Damian winked at Mark. "Luckily, my host has been with you all day, so I have the perfect alibi."

Mark frowned. It was beyond lucky, if he hadn't witnessed it for himself, he would definitely have cast Robert as the villain behind this damage. "Who…?"

"There have been no dark witches, and I can't think of any new demon in the area – we can be quite... territorial." Robert lowered his voice. "There's only one with a grudge."

"Silvaticus?" Mark hissed. "No, he's-"

"A good guy? On your side?" Robert mused, a bitter smile playing across his lips. "Stop thinking about him in quaint human terms. He's a *demon*."

Mark broke off from what he was going to say, when movement caught his eye. Damian's Aunt Maggie was moving hesitantly towards them. She was still shaking from the adrenaline, and her eyes had a frantic look about them.

"I don't understand, has Damian been learning witchcraft, too?" She demanded. "Why would you hide it from me? My *girlfriend* is a witch, I'm totally c-cool about it."

Mark's stomach dropped. He hadn't thought about the consequences of Robert stepping up and doing his thing in public.

Robert simply raised a brow at the brewing drama.

Aunt Maggie grabbed his sleeve, peering at him closer. The differences between Robert and Damian's aura were probably causing her to be further unsettled.

"Your eyes, what's wrong with them?" She screeched, her fingers tightening on her 'nephew's' arm.

Sensing the growing danger, Miriam made her way over, her shoulders slumped as she connected the dots.

"Miriam, what's wrong with his eyes? I've seen you cast spells a hundred times… this isn't right." Aunt Maggie rounded on her girlfriend.

Miriam blanched. All of her energy had been poured into containing the fire, and her eyes silently begged Maggie to let it go.

"Miss Cole, there's something you need to know about Damian." Mark said slowly, his heart breaking that he was sharing Damian's secret. "Do you remember last winter, when he kept saying he was cursed?"

"Yes, but it was a natural reaction, after he'd lost so many loved ones, so quickly." Aunt Maggie said, a little calmer now she was discussing facts. "He even ran away when I had a little accident with the stove, he thought I was going to die too."

Mark remembered that day vividly, when a spell had led him through a snowstorm to rescue Damian. He'd been willing to die, rather than allow his curse to hurt anyone else. Mark shuddered at the mere memory. "Well, he was cursed – sort of. A demon was behind all his grief. It… possessed him. Maggie, I want you to meet Robert."

"No. This is a sick joke." Aunt Maggie snapped. "It's Damian, I can see him as plain as day."

"The demon shares Damian's body. There are very few physical differences when Robert is in control – the black eyes being the main one." Mark tried to explain, but even as he spoke, he could see that he wasn't getting through to Damian's aunt.

"No!"

"It's true, love." Miriam added wearily. "The witches have been trying to expel him, unsuccessfully thus far."

"You knew about this?" Maggie shrieked. "Oh my god, a demon was in *my house*?"

"You were never going to be in any harm, the coven sent me to watch him." Miriam said, trying to pacify her girlfriend.

"You... *what*? Is that what this is? You've just been playing 'happy families' as a duty to your coven?"

"No, Maggs, it's not like that..."

Mark felt a pang of sympathy for Miriam, but knew that anything he said would probably just add fuel to the fire.

Robert looked thoroughly unimpressed by the lover's tiff, pulling his sleeve free from Maggie's grip, he strode away.

Keeping a demon company suddenly seemed more appealing than the very-public domestic argument that was brewing, and Mark jogged to catch up to Robert. "I've been telling Damian for ages to tell his aunt. She'll be OK, won't she?"

Robert gave a patronising huff. "Oddly, I do not concern myself with the emotional state of humans."

"Sorry, I just thought with your experience of revealing the truth about demons to people... this is about normal?" Mark stopped himself from rambling. "Where are you going?"

"To confirm who is trying to frame me, and what his master plan is." Damian replied. "Going after Silvaticus head on is never a good option."

Mark thought back to the battle between Robert and Silvaticus' stone beast at Ostara. No, Mark wouldn't want that stone beast as an enemy. Hadn't Michelle mentioned that Silvaticus was stronger than Robert?

"Maybe I could speak with him." Mark offered.

Robert gave him an odd look. "Maybe, if everything else fails. I have some contacts I need to see. I'll take the demon road, and have your boyfriend back by dawn, so you can go on that shopping trip."

Mark flushed a little, at what else Robert might have seen or heard whilst 'unconscious'. "Do you want me to come?"

"No, I might have to be unpleasant. Besides, I thought you had to stay clear of London?"

Chapter Sixteen

The next morning, Mark woke early. Well, to be honest, he hadn't really slept after yesterday's madness.

He checked his phone, it was now 5:30 am, which meant it was officially Sunday morning. Mark made sure to get up quietly, not wanting to wake his parents. He'd happily face dark witches and demons, but his Mum pre-Coffee was a thing best avoided.

Damian hadn't messaged him, to confirm he was alright after Robert's trip last night. The demon had promised to get his boyfriend home safe, but Mark was far from trusting him. He fired off a text, knowing that if Damian was alright, he was likely fast asleep.

Mark crept downstairs, avoiding the creaky steps as best he could. He grabbed some breakfast from the kitchen, then shuffled into the dark living room. He dropped down onto the sofa, and immediately leapt back up, spilling cereal everywhere.

"Oi!" A familiar girl's voice snapped from beneath the fleece blanket.

"Michelle! You gave me a bloody heart attack!" Mark snapped back. "You know you're in the wrong house?"

"Funny, I hadn't noticed." Michelle said drily. "After their little domestic yesterday, Miriam ended up sleeping on Nanna's sofa."

"And that meant you had to sleep on *our sofa*... why?"

"It started with Nanna and Miriam drinking copious amounts of wine." Michelle yawned and rubbed her sleep-deprived eyes. "Which led to karaoke at 2:00 am, and Nanna booty calling her farrier. He didn't come over, but the conversation was very loud. Nothing the dark witches did to you compares to that torture."

"Well, I need to speak to Miriam about what happened yesterday. We could go repay the favour and wake them up now." Mark shrugged. "Or I can make you some breakfast."

Michelle pursed her lips, considering her options. "Will there be bacon?"

"Sure."

Mark carried his cereal back into the kitchen, suddenly it had lost its appeal against the promise of bacon butties. He started warming the pan on the stove, and pulled the bacon out of the fridge. Mark slid the bread and butter in Michelle's direction, figuring that even in her sleep-deprived state, she should be able to manage getting it ready.

Turning back to the stove, Mark noticed his phone blinking with a new message. He had a moment of relief, before he realised it wasn't his boyfriend replying. Instead, it was an error – 'unable to send message'.

"What's up?" Michelle asked, when it became clear that the bacon was not going into the pan.

"Um, maybe nowt. I tried to text Damian, and it didn't work." Mark replied, with a stab of unease.

"Well, that's not uncommon, signal is shite up here." Michelle's sharp comments managed to be helpful. "Why don't you ring his home phone?"

"At 5:30 in the morning?"

"'Kay, maybe not *right now*." Michelle shrugged. "If you're worried about Robert getting him back home, you could do a location spell. Have you got owt belonging to Damian?"

Mark paused. "Yeah, I think I've got some stuff in my room."

He headed back upstairs, careful to keep as quiet as possible. He didn't need to worry his parents yet. Mark went into his room and rummaged through the mess until he found Damian's red hoody.

He held it close for a moment, telling himself that he was just overreacting, and that Damian would be tucked up in bed.

Mark took the hoody back to the kitchen, surprised to find Michelle at the stove, midway through cooking the bacon.

"I thought you were allergic to using the stove." He teased.

Michelle stuck her tongue out in response. "Get your spell done quick, this'll be ready in a few minutes.

Mark sat at the breakfast bar and grabbed some bits to represent the four corners. A pot of rosemary, glass of water, an empty bowl and a candle. They all came together to create a circle. Even this early in the morning, Mark could feel his magic respond, his own fear and worry fading away as he found his natural balance.

Mark held Damian's top in both hands, and focussed his will on finding his boyfriend.

"North, South, East, West;

"Listen to my will;

"Lift the veil;

"Show me who I seek."

The water lifted from the bowl and shimmered across the table in a thin, crystalline layer. It hovered for a moment, before splashing down onto the surface.

Mark frowned. He really wasn't having any luck with these location spells. First, the one he did in London exploded in his face; now this one just… failed.

"So, where is he?" Michelle asked, setting down a plate of bacon butties in front of Mark.

"It didn't work." Mark replied numbly.

"What? What did you do?"

Mark explained the spell, which only caused Michelle to look more confused.

"Well it worked perfectly for me, when you buggered off the other week." Michelle frowned. "Do y'want me to try?"

Mark moved out the way, so Michelle could have a go. The girl repeated his actions, repeated the words... and got the same result.

"I don't understand, that worked last time." Michelle bit her lip.

"Let's wake Nanna and Miriam, so we can ask their advice." Mark suggested.

"Yes!" Michelle agreed, a little too eagerly.

Mark chuckled as he pulled on his coat. Together they traipsed next door, and let themselves into Nanna's side of the house. There were empty wine bottles on the table, and empty ice cream cartons littering the work surface. Signs of a heavy 'girl's night in'. Mark would bet anything they had Bridget Jones in the DVD player.

"Nanna?" He called upstairs.

There was the sound of movement above them, muffled swearing, and feet slowly hitting the floor.

"D'you have any idea what time it is?" Nanna shouted back.

"Yeah." Mark answered, slightly amused at the hungover mess that was his Nanna. "We both tried a location spell, and couldn't get it to work."

Nanna made her way downstairs, wrapped in her fluffy pink dressing gown. Her hair was a wild mess, and her eyes had that staring quality that could only come after a night of drink and no sleep. Her eyes turned to the clock. "What'cha doin' spells at bloody 5:30 for?"

"Some of us couldn't sleep." Michelle said pointedly.

Unfortunately, the point went straight over Nanna's befuddled head.

"I wanted to check that Robert delivered Damian home last night, like he promised." Mark said, making sure to use short words.

"Ugh, demon promises? Flimsy things." Nanna groaned.

She shuffled around the kitchen, clearing some of the mess from the table. Once there was a surface to work on, she went through the same steps for a location spell, and sat looking stumped.

"What does that mean?" Mark asked.

"It means someone is blocking our spells – unlikely – even when a powerful witch like Edith tried to interfere with your spell in London, it didn't stop it entirely." Nanna yawned, rubbing her bloodshot eyes. "Something demonic is blocking our spell – possible, but unlikely. Robert is one of the strongest demons we've encountered. Finally, he's somewhere out of reach of the location spell – maybe he's in the demon realm, you did say he was taking a trip via the demon road."

"Yes, but he was only going to London, and he's supposed to be back by now." Mark argued.

"Then call his aunt. Sometimes the non-magical route is the answer." Nanna grumbled, making a beeline for the kettle and her morning coffee.

Mark checked his watch. It was nearly 6am. Before he could wuss out, he rang Damian's landline. Two rings, three. Maybe it would just go through to the answer machine.

"Hullo?" A woman's voice answered.

"Miss Cole? It's Mark."

"Mark? Oh, thank god. Is Damian with you? Can you tell him I didn't mean-"

"No, he's not here." Mark interrupted; his worst fears confirmed. "I was just checking if he got home OK, he's not answering his phone."

There was a sob on the other end of the line. "I've pushed him away again, haven't I? Just when he needed... I just freaked out when a demon was mentioned, now I've lost them both..."

"Miriam is here, a little worse for wear." Mark said. "And we're going to find Damian and bring him home again."

Mark looked up, to see both Michelle and Nanna watching him carefully, frowning at his side of the conversation.

"I've got to go, Miss Cole. We'll be in touch when we know owt." Mark said, wrapping up the conversation, before Damian's aunt could blame herself any further.

The three witches sat in silence, the only noise the whistling kettle.

"W-what about the spell we used to find E-Eadric?" Mark asked hesitantly, stumbling over the name of his late friend. This was the first time he had mentioned him unprompted, and it just felt wrong to speak of him. "That was strong enough to cross through time. Maybe it could work across realms."

"Not a bad idea." Nanna tilted her head. "We do have four witches to hand."

"A big spell?" Michelle perked up. "I'm up for that."

"The first thing we need is coffee, very strong coffee; or two of your witches may fall asleep."

Laden with coffee and toast, they broached the living room. The only sign of life was the sound of snoring that came from a ball of blankets and duvets on the couch.

Miriam was in even a worse state than Nanna, a zombie in the making. She didn't say a word, and her eyes lost all focus, but she obediently drank the coffee that was thrust into her hands.

Mark bit back a smile at how poorly these supposed-adults coped with their problems. But then he remembered how much his own heart had hurt when Damian had broken it. If he'd had access to alcohol to numb the pain, he might have done the same. Instead, he ran into the moors like he was in an Emily Bronte novel, and he'd met someone who made him feel better, just for a while…

"Earth to Mark." Michelle snapped.

Mark instinctively raised his hands to defend against whatever she was about to throw, and was surprised to find that Michelle was lacking missiles.

As the house was too cramped to make a decent circle, the four witches filed out into the garden. A refreshing morning breeze blew steadily, helping to make Nanna and Miriam more alert.

Mark moved to face Nanna, and waited for the others to form the circle. As soon as Miriam and Michelle took their places, their magic flowed together in a now-familiar rhythm. The power swirled within the circle, quickly building upon itself, as all the witches worked together.

Out of curiosity, Mark let his attention drift to Miriam. They were in the same coven, but Mark had only worked in large groups with her, Miriam's signature lost in the crowd. Ignoring last night's fiasco with the demon-fuelled magic, this was the first time Mark had been able to take note of Miriam's magic. It wasn't as strong as some of the other witches he had worked with; but Mark was surprised to see how much it was fuelled by her emotions. She always seemed so composed on the surface, but Mark could see deep feelings that were the strongest part of her core.

Mark didn't want to look too closely at Michelle's magic. He thought it would be an intrusion, but even brushing against her in the circle, he was amazed at her potential for power. It shouldn't have come as a shock, after all her mother was strong, and Nanna was always talking about the power of bloodlines.

Within the circle, their magic continued to thicken, so much potential, awaiting direction.

Mark glanced up, waiting too, for Nanna to lead the way, as she had the last time they performed this spell. She seemed sluggish in wielding the magic before them, and Mark wondered if it was his imagination, now that he knew about her illness, but he thought he saw a crack in her cloak of power.

Before things could get out of hand, Mark began to chant the spell.

"Through the mists of time and space;

"Through locks and walls, to this set place.

"We call upon the ancient power;

"Greeted at the midnight hour.

"Link our hopes and hearts as one;

"Til our intentions be done."

Mark heard the other witches echo the spell, their magic combining and flowing back to him. Mark's knees nearly buckled, as the magic overwhelmed his senses and responded to *him*. There was a moment when the power accepted him, recognised him as the natural heir to the Grand High Witch.

Mark tried to float above the dizzying sensation. He opened his eyes and turned his intentions into the circle, where the air thickened to a dark grey. There were vague moving shapes, that started to sharpen in the vision.

Mark's heart dropped when he saw the result of the spell. His question answered, the magic broke out of the circle, flowing over the four witches.

"I don't understand, it didn't even show Damian. Just a hunk of rock." Michelle said, her pupils dilated from the rush. "Did you screw up that spell, too?"

"It showed where he is. I recognise the location." Mark replied quietly. "Brimcliff prison… it probably deflects external spells… on top of everything else."

"Brimcliff? As in the *demon prison* in the *demon realm*?" Michelle hissed back. "Why is he there?"

'Why' was easy – Robert was an escaped convict. According to the other demons, that's where he belonged. *'How'* was another question; and how they were getting Damian out was another.

Mark's attention was caught by his Nanna. The late night and the big spell looked like they had been too much for her. She looked scarily pale, and Mark dashed forward, as her knees started to buckle.

Mark caught her and scooped her into his arms. She was surprisingly light. He carried Nanna back into the house, and laid her down on the sofa. She was still breathing, but her pulse was light.

Miriam stumbled against the furniture, eyes locked on Nanna, looking completely terrified. She was in no place to help her unconscious coven leader.

"Miriam, can you go into the kitchen, heat up some of Nanna's magic tea. She keeps some in the fridge."

The woman nodded numbly, and made her way noisily into the kitchen.

Mark glanced at Michelle. "Do you know any healing spells?"

Michelle shook her head mutely.

Mark sighed, trying to keep calm and in control, as a thought began to niggle. "I'll teach you one. Might be useful."

He sat on the floor next to Nanna, and placed a hand on her arm. Closing his eyes, he began to recite.

"Hear my will, take my strength;

"Bind the wounds, and heal the flesh;

"Honour my words;

"Secure this life."

The last time Mark had used this spell was to save a restaurant full of people that Robert had tried to suffocate. Healing one person was much easier, and Mark felt the flow of magic was much stronger. Whether Mark was becoming better at this witch thing, or the magic was fuelled by his emotional connection to Nanna, Mark could only guess. It seemed to take only moments, before Mark started to see the results. Colour returned to Nanna's cheeks, and her pulse strengthened.

Miriam came shuffling back in, and breathed a sigh of relief at the visible improvement. She held up a mug of steaming tea. "I… was this my fault? Did I push Nanna too much last night?"

Mark shook his head. He wasn't sure if Nanna had told anyone else about her health issues. "It's not your fault Miriam. Have you ever known Nanna to do more or less than she precisely desires?"

Miriam gave a snort and her lips tilted slightly, in an awkward, almost-smile.

Mark got up and backed away from the sofa, gesturing for Michelle to follow him outside. Although early, the day was warming up to be a lovely summer's day, a complete contrast to all the drama that was starting.

"You OK?" Michelle asked, without a trace of her usual sarcasm.

His boyfriend was locked in a demon prison, and his powerful Nanna had been wiped out by a relatively simple spell. "I'm fine."

Michelle bit her lip, but at least didn't call bollocks on his statement. "What now?"

"I go get Damian."

"How?" Michelle frowned. "You can't trust Silvaticus, he's the only demon who knew where Robert was. He's also the only demon that can take you to their realm."

Mark nodded, he'd had the same suspicions about the demon that was supposed to be their ally. Had Silvaticus been so keen to get revenge on Robert, he'd broken his promises to Mark; and sacrificed Robert's innocent host? "There's another way."

Michelle's eyes widened, as she realised what he was talking about. "No, you can't use dark magic. It's not worth it."

"It's the only way." Mark replied, calm now he'd made his mind up. "I love Damian. I'm not letting him rot in a demon prison."

"Then I'll do it. I'm more familiar with dark magic, and there's no point it wrecking us both."

Mark stared in surprise, that was perhaps the nicest thing Michelle had said to date. He grabbed her hand. "No, we don't know if you'll come back from using dark magic again. I need you to stay here and protect Nanna."

"You're really stubborn."

Mark gave a bitter smile. "It runs in the family."

Michelle stepped back towards the house, and then stopped, rounding on Mark. "If you insist on being the hero, please get changed. I don't want to tell people that you saved the day in your pyjamas."

Chapter Seventeen

Mark took Michelle's advice, and swapped the wrinkled pyjamas for jeans and, remembering how cold Brimcliff Duchy was, he grabbed a winter coat.

Mark jogged down the garden, heading for the empty field beyond. It helped to burn off his nerves, and stop him from thinking about what a stupid idea this was.

He finally stopped, looked back at the house and, taking a deep breath, he tentatively reached out. "*Síþwegas*."

There was a familiar flash of light, followed by the red nothingness of the demon road. Mark held his breath, so utterly focussed on steering the road to the gate nearest the Brimcliff Duchy. Mark only breathed again when another flash of light signalled the end of his journey, revealing the empty moors of the demon realm.

As the spell connecting him to the road was complete, the dark magic reluctantly pulled back. Mark glanced at his arms, sure it would leave a visible sticky residue, but his skin was bare.

Mark took a deep breath, unable to shake the unnatural feeling of this place. It was even more forbidding without Silvaticus for company. The unchanging sameness of this in-between was so unsettling. The sooner he got Damian and got out, the better.

Mark closed his eyes as he attempted his second piece of dark magic – he had many more ahead, and really should stop counting… "*Mēaras*."

Mark's knees shook at the sensation, the power rippled through him, with so much seductive potential it was hard for him to concentrate.

His balance was further challenged when the ground began to rumble in response to his spell. Mark fell on his arse, he was glad he didn't have a witness to his embarrassment.

The earth in front of him began to bubble up, and Mark waited, expecting to see the huge stone horses that Silvaticus had summoned. He scrambled to his feet as something akin to hot magma emerged.

Backing away to safety, Mark tried to take it in. The animal looked horse-like. Its limbs were grey, but the rest of the body blazed with red and orange fire. In the flickering light, it looked like it had grey stone for a skeleton, beneath the fiery flesh.

Despite its terrifying appearance, the animal stood placidly, waiting for its next command.

Mark approached tentatively, hand held out, as he would to a nervous horse; but the creature looked at him with empty eyes, not moving a muscle.

Mark put a hand on the horse's shoulder. It was warmer than the stone beasts, but despite the flame, it didn't burn him.

"Lie down." He said, nervously. "Please."

The horse immediately lay down, its limbs tucked awkwardly under its body.

Mark gingerly climbed across its back, but the horse didn't show any reaction. "Stand."

The horse lumbered to its feet so quickly, that Mark nearly tumbled off. He leant forward, and clung to the dark red mane. It was almost uncomfortably warm in his hands, but not as hot as he feared.

"Can you take me to Brimcliff prison?" Mark asked. "Please?"

The horse shot off at a gallop, keeping a steady pace regardless of the undulating terrain; and never tiring. The horse was a finer build than the ones Silvaticus had summoned, and reminded Mark of his Nanna's horse, Lulu. Despite the skinnier frame, the fiery flesh was softer and more comfortable than the stone version.

Mark assumed the spell responded differently to different users. Silvaticus' strongest element was stone, it seemed natural that would appear in his spells. It wasn't as if Mark could go ask him right now. His stomach gave another bitter twist at Silvaticus' potential betrayal.

Travelling alone, the journey seemed to take forever. With no visual marker for where the Brimcliff Duchy started, it was hard to keep track of how long they'd been at it, and how long they had left.

Mark sighed, his hand resting on the horse's neck. "I wish you could go faster."

The creature snorted through its stony nostrils, spraying droplets of lava; the first noise it had made. The fire shifted beneath Mark, and with no warning, it burst out of the shoulders in a giant fan of orange sparks.

Mark gripped his knees tighter, worried that he'd accidentally triggered a jet-powered mode. He hadn't meant-

The horse's speed increased, it bunched its fiery muscles up and leapt off the ground. Mark waited for the hooves to hit the track again, but the moor scrubland looked further and further away. There was a jerky movement, as the great orange extensions moved up and down, finding a new rhythm.

"Wings, you've got wings..." Mark said faintly, before swearing harsh enough to make Nanna blush.

Once he'd gotten over his shock, Mark whooped loudly, then laughed as he tried to find the best position for riding a *flying horse*. Oh, he so wished he could bring this home. The others were going to be so jealous when he told them (except for Harry, who was afraid of heights).

As they flew over the land, it looked as boring as ever, but at least they were flying. They moved at such speed that the wind whipped tears from Mark's eyes; but if it were any colder, Mark couldn't tell, riding this furnace of a flying horse.

It felt like time was also flying, and Mark could just see the shimmer that marked the boundary of the Brimcliff Duchy. This time he didn't have time to feel nervous, and it was behind him in no time.

The sudden change was a shock to his system. Frigid air rushed into his lungs, and the daylight faded to leave total darkness. The horse was so bright, Mark's eyes struggled to make out the shadowy world below them.

Mark flexed his stiff fingers, and wrapped them tighter in the horse's mane. "Take me to the prison." Mark ordered.

The fiery horse altered its trajectory, tilting away to Mark's right, and starting to descend. They got low enough that Mark could see the grey buildings, and the milling of demons and pale trapped souls along the paths. It all looked tiny and so far away, but Mark was sure everyone was stopping to look up at their arrival. On second thought, this probably wasn't the most subtle way to approach the prison; but Mark was still flooded with dark magic, his judgement impaired. He shrugged it off – let them look. He would be done with his mission in no time.

Mark leant close to the horse's neck and urged it faster towards the prison. He could see the hulk of rock jutting out from the violent seas. As they drew closer, he could taste the salt water in the air about them.

The horse flew over the rickety dock, and headed obediently over the open water, closing the distance. Mark asked it to aim for the top of the prison. He would try and find a way in from-

The world turned upside down.

There was silence, as the water pulled back, and then it roared up, a titan swatting at a pesky fly. Mark was vaguely aware of the wall of water, a fraction of a second before it pummelled him. It was cold, and hard, and knocked his limbs about like a ragdoll. Mark tried to grip onto his horse, but couldn't sense where the beast was. He started to panic, he needed air, but when his mouth opened, there was only cold, foul-tasting water.

He felt blackness creeping in, and then everything seemed to stop.

Mark choked and coughed up the water that had tried to drown him. Mark opened his eyes, the salt stinging, but he could see a rocky shore. There was loose shingle that shifted underneath him, the sharp edges cutting his hands. He'd been lucky not to be seriously hurt in that fall – he couldn't remember doing any magic to protect himself…

Mark gingerly sat up, feeling like every inch of him was bruised. As his gaze lifted higher, he saw… a pair of dainty white pumps. Mark looked up to see the odd demon he'd spotted during his trip with Silvaticus. She had pale blonde hair, tied back with a blue ribbon that matched her blue skirt, and white frilly shirt.

"You ninny, you can't broach the prison with dark magic." The girl said, her voice light and oddly happy, despite her chiding.

"What happened?" Mark asked, his voice hoarse.

"Incy wincy spider climbed up the waterspout, down came the rain and washed the spider out…" The girl had a bright and perfect smile. "Naughty human, there is only one way in."

Mark frowned. He wondered if he'd had a concussion, and this was all some weird hallucination. "You're… a demon?"

"Yes." The girl replied in a sing song voice.

"Are you… am I in trouble? Or are you helping me?"

"Yes." The girl repeated.

Mark blinked. 'Yes'? Which part was that answer directed to? If given the choice, he'd be optimistic. "Why are you helping me?"

The girl tilted her head to one side, looking the picture of innocence. "Luka likes you. He says you are one of the good ones, and you are not allowed to get stuck here."

Mark was not expecting that. This demon had to be a hallucination brewed up by his battered brain; how else could she know about his protective spirit. Mark got unsteadily to his feet, wincing at the sprained ankle and shoulder that screamed in silent agony.

"I have to save my boyfriend; I'm not leaving him behind." Mark insisted. "Can you help me get into the prison?"

"There is one way in, ninny." The demon shook her head at his silly forgetfulness. "Once inside the prison, all demons are powerless. They dream, they pray, they curse; such a sad song."

"Please, is there anything you can do to help?"

"I will catch you… no, *caught you*. That already happened." The girl bit her pink lip, thinking very hard. She stepped forward and put a hand on Mark's arm.

If Mark hadn't been in so much pain, he would have jumped back. Instead, he stood looking at the ghostly pale hand on his tattered sleeve. The girl's magic started to course over his whole body. Mark closed his eyes, in awe of how much raw power was hidden behind this strange person.

He felt a lightness in his limbs, she was *healing* him.

Her magic felt odd, so very different to the dark magic that he'd seen other demons and dark witches use. It lacked the cloying, addictiveness; and when the spell finished, Mark felt refreshed and *clean* of the demon realm's tendrils.

"Who are you?" He asked nervously.

"My friends call me Mel." The girl announced with a dazzling smile.

Without another word, she vanished.

Chapter Eighteen

Mark jumped; the girl had disappeared without having to use the demon road… further evidence that he really knew nothing about the rules in this place. He pushed back the fear of being in over his head, and looked down the rocky shore towards the prison.

His horse had been destroyed in the wave. Mark couldn't see any signs of it, the creature of fire and stone was lost to the sea; but he could feel it. The spell had ended, the connection gone.

The strange demon girl had said there was only one way into the prison; and for some reason, Mark didn't doubt the truth of her words for a minute. There had been an innocent honesty about her, that was hard to shake.

Following Mel's advice, he headed towards the rickety dock, his ankle no longer hurting, and his shoulder fine.

When he got there, the scaled boatman looked at him with intense, unblinking eyes.

"Can you take me to the prison?" Mark asked, tentatively.

The boatman's forked tongue flashed out, and he tilted his head slightly, continuing to observe the human.

Mark waited, but was getting no further response. Maybe that was a 'yes'? He gingerly stepped into the boat. After all, the worst that could happen was he could take another swim; and he was already soaking wet.

The boat rocked a little beneath his feet, but didn't immediately throw him into the sea. The boatman turned to his rudder and steered the boat away from shore, heading to the prison.

The great rock monolith that made up the prison looked twice as daunting from the sea-level, as it had from the back of his flying horse. As they moved into its impressive shadow, it felt inevitable and inescapable. Mark had been a fool to try and break in; he would have to try and negotiate with the Governor. He remembered how the Governor had watched him last time, perhaps there was a deal Mark could make.

The boat rocked up to the single door of the prison, and when Mark stepped towards it, a golem guard appeared. The grey, featureless face turned towards Mark expectantly.

"I'm here to see the Governor." Mark announced.

The golem paused, relaying the information to its master then nodded. They unlocked the iron door and held it open for Mark.

Mark hesitated at the dark entrance, walking into the inescapable prison was foolhardy, but he couldn't leave Damian to rot. He took a deep breath of salty air, and stepped inside.

As the door was locked behind him, Mark felt as though a limb had been chopped off. He'd been using dark magic for a couple of hours, and without thinking, he had kept connected to it, like he did with natural magic. It was now gone, yanked away without warning, leaving Mark staggering against the stone wall, as pain and shock ran through him.

Shit, he'd only been borrowing that dark magic for a brief period. He couldn't imagine how much torment it would cause a demon to step foot in here. He couldn't remember Silvaticus giving any sign that it had hurt him during their visit, but that demon had cool and collected down to an art.

As for the prisoners... Mark could hear them, he could feel their anguish, before he could see them. It was even worse than he remembered. The cries and moans of pain struck to his very bones, making him shiver.

He walked down the corridor, and the cells came into view. Demons lay in their cells, all so very different, with two legs, four legs, wings or tentacles; but they were all the same with the despair in their eyes. They were never getting out.

Mark wondered how long some of them had been locked away in here. No matter their crimes, was the punishment worth it? From what Mark could work out, Robert had been in here for thirty years. Since his escape, he still couldn't be trusted, but hadn't he shown that he could act like the better man? Or… demon?

Try as he might, his thoughts couldn't distract from the prison around him. Mark was relieved when he found a familiar wooden door. He shoved it open, to see the same messy office that they had visited previously. The Governor hovered behind their desk, and smiled when she saw Mark, baring a set of sharp teeth.

"Well, well. Tired of Silvaticus already? I can't blame you, he's awfully uptight." The Governor licked her lips, her black eyes sparkling with interest.

"There seems to have been a misunderstanding." Mark said, trying to sound more confident than he felt. "When we were last here, you agreed to stop hunting Robert. Yet he was taken last night."

"You poor innocent fool." The Governor chuckled, her whole body rippling with restrained mirth. "You have much to learn about demon agreements. I agreed to stop hunting him with *hell beasts*. We didn't stop altogether."

Mark felt a heavy weight in his stomach. "But… Silvaticus promised Damian wouldn't get hurt. You can keep Robert, but release Damian."

"Silvaticus was not in a position to make such a promise." The Governor shook her head. "And we cannot separate the demon from his human host. When demons come to us in this form, we wait for their hosts to die in about seventy years, then continue the sentence for eternity."

"Damian doesn't deserve this." Mark's voice shook. "If Robert is going to be here for eternity, surely you can release them to my custody for those seventy years. Or at least give my coven a chance to separate the demon and host."

The Governor looked amused. "We have rules, young witch. Why would I flout them?"

"I'll soon be the Grand High Witch: a powerful ally for you to have. I'll do anything it takes."

"While I'd like to trust that statement, there's nothing I can do now." One of the creature's tentacles flicked up close by Mark's face, making him flinch. "You humans aren't bound by honesty, like demons. I can't trust what you say, and I will not release such a high-profile prisoner on a flimsy promise."

Mark sighed, not sure what he could do.

"Although, I will accept payment up front. You will work for me until the debt is settled, then I will release your human for… whatever years of life he has left." The Governor offered, her sharp teeth showing again.

Mark suspected that was the best offer he was going to get from this shrewd demon. He noticed that the Governor had failed to mention how long it would take, and the amount of debt that would need to be written off – probably on purpose. Would Mark ever free Damian?

Mark nodded, "Um… can I see Damian before I leave?"

The Governor pulled back her tendril, her eyes shining with thoughts that Mark didn't want to know.

"Very well. Down the hall, stairs to the right. Come back here before you leave, and we can discuss our… arrangement further."

Mark backed out of the room, not wanting to turn his back on the Governor. He couldn't wait to put some distance between them, the way her greedy eyes fed on him was just disturbing.

He followed her instructions, finding the stairs. They went up steeply, with uneven steps. Mark kept his hand on the wall, to stop himself tripping, and to steel himself against going further into this prison. Small lanterns dotted the corridor, their green fire casting a weak, sickly light.

Robert's cell was in the top corner of the prison, one of the furthest from the only exit; they clearly didn't want to risk him escaping again. Mark passed a cell with an innocent-looking horse creature, which lay limply against the bars. It flinched as Mark went by, and blue eyes followed him.

Mark tried to ignore the despair in the other prisoners in this high-security section. He focussed on the slumped figure in the furthest cell. His blonde hair seemed dull, his skin was pale and littered with bruises. His clothes were rumpled and stained black with dried blood.

Mark knelt on the floor, he looked even worse close up.

His eyes flickered open, and Mark could see the black iris'. He didn't know why, but he was somewhat grateful that Robert was the conscious one right now. Mark shuddered at the thought of his gentle and empathetic boyfriend having to cope with the pain of everyone around him.

"Robert?"

"This is an interesting form of torture. Are you going to kill him in front of me? Or is he going to beat me next?" Robert's voice was hoarse, and a little muffled from a swollen split lip. "I'm not going to fall for your illusions, Governor. You know me better than that."

"Robert, it's really me." Mark insisted.

"F-forgive me if I don't believe you." Robert replied, trying to make a dismissive gesture with his hand, but his arm spasmed in pain. "Mark would never come here for me."

Mark bit his tongue. He wouldn't wish this prison on his worst enemy, but he couldn't honestly say, if Robert were stuck here alone, whether he would make any attempt to help him. "Can you believe I'm here for Damian? I told you, I love him. He doesn't deserve to rot in here."

"No, he doesn't..." Robert looked at Mark curiously, trying to weigh up if he was real.

"What happened to you?" Mark asked.

"They didn't appreciate the fact that I escaped." Robert took a shuddering breath. "I've... kept Damian's consciousness subdued. I'm growing quite fond of that wet rag, and he shouldn't have to face my torture."

"Thank you." Mark frowned, he hadn't expected Robert to give Damian such consideration.

Robert watched the emotions playing across Mark's face. "It's really you? How are you here?" This time his voice shook with something other than pain.

"Long story. The Governor wants me to work for them for an unspecified amount of time, before she'll consider releasing you. I need some better options." Mark gazed at Robert. "How did you escape last time?"

"I had to wait a decade for a human to summon me, then I had to wait until his son turned sixteen..." Robert licked his dry lips, gesturing to the body he inhabited. "But I was in my demon form that time. If I tried it again, I would leave this body behind, and your beloved Damian would be left to handle this without my protection."

"Not really an option." Mark agreed.

"Give me another thirty years, I might change my mind." Robert gave a humourless smile.

Mark leant against the bars and sighed. "Are there any... dark magic spells... that could help?"

Robert looked at him again, probably seeing the tell-tale signs of dark magic usage all over his skin. Mark felt positively dirty.

"Well, well. What a hypocrite. If you'd just used dark magic when I requested, instead of summoning Silvaticus, we wouldn't be in this mess." Robert tutted his disapproval. "This prison blocks dark magic. Only the Governor keeps their power."

"Believe me, this is a one off. I'm going back to natural magic, and sticking to it."

"Do you have to be so painfully *good*?" Robert asked.

Mark wasn't listening, his own thoughts were occupying his whole attention. He couldn't wait to get back home, where he could access his light magic. Silvaticus had warned him that it wouldn't work here, as there was nothing natural in the demon realm.

But… *he* was natural. He had natural magic coursing through his blood, he had the elements in every cell in his body. He was the grandson of the Grand High Witch, that had to count for something?

Even as Mark's head told him it was an insane train of thought, his heart encouraged him that he was right. It occurred to him that the odd demon girl had been very careful in her words – she had said there was only one *way in,* which perhaps meant there was *another way out.*

He closed his eyes and meditated, calling on the corners. Nothing happened at first, he struggled like a new witch who'd never cast a spell; but then it flickered to light within him. Small, and fragile, he nurtured the spark of magic within him.

When he opened his eyes, Mark found Robert staring at him intently.

"Well... that's new." The demon mumbled, excitement brightening his black eyes.

"Why did you need me to use dark magic?" Mark asked suddenly.

"What?"

"I'm not going to let you out, if you're planning on hurting people. I need to know what your master plan is." Mark pointed out.

Robert groaned and looked away from him.

"There was nothing *devious*. I'd been locked down here for thirty years – a pathetically short time, but I'd lost most of my human allies to *old age*. I've always tracked down powerful young witches, like you and Michelle; converted them to dark magic. Both parties win, the witches gain more power, and I gain loyal followers." Robert broke off and turned back to face Mark. "And you, my dear, were going to be the shining star in my collection. Such a shame you chose the boring route."

"Sounds pretty devious to me." Mark muttered. "Why do you even need witches, you're a powerful demon?"

"Because I'm not the only powerful demon out there. Silvaticus was always stronger; I had to make up the deficit in any way I could..."

"Well, things are different now. They have to be." Mark insisted. "You can't make anyone use dark magic again. You can't hurt anyone."

"Agreed." Robert said quietly, without flinching.

Mark didn't move. He knew that demon promises were more binding than human ones, but that all seemed too easy, he still didn't trust Robert as far as he could throw him.

Robert read his hesitation, and smiled bitterly. "Ah, of course. I have given you no reason to trust me. I could try charming you, but so far you seem immune to my attempts. Come closer."

Before he could think any better of it, Mark leant closer to the demon. Close enough to feel the heat of Robert's skin, and his breath on his neck.

The demon breathed a single word. One that had such weight, that Mark didn't doubt the meaning of it. The demon's name.

The demon looked at him with a strange expression. "Are we good?"

"Yeah… yeah, we are." Mark replied.

He staggered to his feet, feeling a little dizzy. Demon names had their own power, and they'd longed to find Robert's true name, so they could expel him from Damian's body.

Mark could do it here and now, knock Robert out, and rescue Damian alone; but his skin crawled at the very thought of doing so.

He connected with that spark of magic, and coaxed it to burn brighter. Aware of how little he had to work with, Mark decided to go for something simple. They were on the top floor, only a wall separating them from the sea. Mark channelled the power to find weaknesses in the rock, allowed the light to corrode the darkness that held those walls together.

It wasn't a fast process, but Mark held steady, terrified that he'd forever lose his connection to the flickering magic.

He knew that he'd been successful when a cold breeze blew against his hot, sweaty skin. The smell of sea salt now prevalent, much preferred to the stale air that had gone before it.

Robert got unsteadily to his feet, and started kicking the loose rock at the corner of his cell, keen to taste his freedom. The lump of stone soon tipped and fell down, down, down to the sea, where the sound of the splash was lost to the waves.

"What is the second step of your plan?" Robert asked, peering at the great drop before them. "I'm in no state to use my magic, and many have died swimming these seas."

"I can fly you back to shore." A hissing voice with a Scottish lilt, came from behind them.

Mark turned to see the horse-like demon was on its feet, suddenly looking a lot more energetic and hopeful than before.

"Release me, and in return, I will take you safe to shore." The demon insisted, its ears twitching back and forth with excitement.

"It's a kelpie; more likely to drop us in the ocean than carry us over it." Robert said dismissively. "You can't trust it."

"Like I shouldn't trust you?" Mark snapped back.

He really wished he'd thought this plan through. Hell, he wished he'd thought any of his plans through, but he'd just been so focussed on rescuing Damian. Now he'd rescued Robert, and was about to free a kelpie.

Mark turned towards the horse-like creature. Its body was black with a sickly green sheen, there was a translucent quality, as it seemed to flicker in and out of sight. "I need… can you promise that me and Robert will arrive on shore, alive and unharmed?"

The kelpie lowered its head, looking pointedly at the other demon. "I swear you will both arrive with no *further* injury."

"I still recommend against…"

Mark tuned out Robert's protest, instead focussing his magic towards the cell that held the kelpie. He could feel the power weakening, he'd only have one chance at this.

The wall fractured and started to crumble when the magic Mark had been using faded away. He swore and started to kick the weakened section.

Despite his protestations, Robert joined him, using his bare hands to help pull lumps of stone away.

"Stand aside." The kelpie hissed.

Mark scrabbled back, pulling Robert with him. A moment later the wall shivered behind a heavy blow. A second blow from the kelpie's back feet, and rock flew at their heads.

Mark stood amongst the rubble the unusual trio had created. The kelpie moved delicately across the floor, looking the picture of innocence.

"Get on."

Mark vaulted onto the back of the kelpie, which felt solid enough, despite the fact that it still kept flickering out of view.

Robert was missing his usual agility, and struggled to mount. Mark ended up having to drag him up.

Without warning, the kelpie dropped out of the gaping hole, plunging down to the seas below.

"We should try staying high, there's some wicked defences." Mark shouted to their steed.

The kelpie hissed at him, taking them lower. The rocks around the base of the prison were sharp and deadly, and getting ever closer.

Mark grabbed the kelpie's seaweed mane, and he felt Robert's arms tighten around his waist.

At the last second, the kelpie veered up, skimming the tops of the waves. The water began to swell and lash out at the escapees.

Mark tightened his knees as the kelpie picked up speed, nimbly dancing between the jets of water that tried to knock them to oblivion. The kelpie was clearly in their element. The constant shifts made Mark feel nauseous, and held his breath, praying for it to end.

In what felt like an eternity later, they reached the shore. The kelpie arched its back, bucking Mark and Robert onto the stony ground.

Feeling more than a little dazed, Mark staggered to his feet. "Thank you, kelpie."

The creature lowered its head. "Thank you, Grand High Witch." It took off, heading north, skipping between the shore and the grey waves.

Mark turned to Robert, who was much slower at getting to his feet. The demon looked exhausted, his skin pale and limbs shaking.

"What do you know, the kelpie let us live." Robert tried to smile.

"Yeah," Mark replied, getting Robert's arm around his shoulder, so he could help support him. They needed to move away from the shore before anyone spotted them. "It seemed so helpful, I wonder why they were locked up."

"It had been killing demon and human children for generations. When they found its lair, it was full of blood and little bones." Robert explained. "They have been locked in that prison for over fifty years."

"What?" Mark's head snapped round, watching the kelpie disappear into the shadows.

He would really have to think about who he allied himself with in future. First, Silvaticus had betrayed him;

now his 'innocent-looking' water creature was anything but.

Robert didn't respond to his exclamation, his concentration solely on putting one step in front of the other. There was no way he was going to walk any distance, and they couldn't stay here. It surely wouldn't be long before the whole of Brimcliff knew about their escape.

"Mēaras."

Mark felt the dark magic leap with joy at being reconnected with him, it surged through his veins in a heady delight, clinging to his skin. The stony ground began to quake and crack, revealing a red-hot glow beneath.

Robert watched silently, as the horse of fire and stone climbed out of the rock, and stood patiently for its creator.

The creature looked identical to the one that had been lost to the sea. Mark half-expected there to be some sort of recognition from the animal, then reminded himself it was just a spell. Its fiery eyes gazed at them neutrally, waiting for his commands.

"Interesting." Robert murmured.

Mark got them both mounted, with Robert in front of him, so he could physically keep him on the horse.

"Get us to the gate." Mark ordered. "Fly."

The horse took a couple of steps, picking up speed, as fire sprouted from its shoulders. With a lurch, they were airborne.

Mark spotted a blonde figure dressed in white in the town below, who calmly watched them leave. He waved a silent thanks to Mel, before he focussed on keeping them both upright.

Chapter Nineteen

They left the Brimcliff Duchy, with no sign of pursuit. The in-between moors went by with a boring consistency.

Robert drifted in and out of consciousness throughout the flight, and Mark clung to him, not wanting to test if the demon could survive a fall from a great height.

Once they reached the gate, it was almost too easy for Mark to direct the road towards Damian's house. They came out in a field, half a mile from the village. After everything that had happened, Mark was shocked to see that it was nearly evening of what seemed to have been a ridiculously long day.

Then the gate closed, and Mark felt like someone had lopped off a limb. He fell to his knees gasping. He'd lost his connection to the steady dark magic from the demon realm. The cloying power that had clung to him like a second skin had been ripped away so violently, Mark was surprised that his arms weren't red and raw. His stomach tipped at the sudden change, and he retched.

Shit. His Nanna had warned him that dark magic was addictive, but he'd only used it for *one day*. Yes, he'd gone in the deep end, but it had still only been a day.

Robert sat slumped in the grass beside him, his injuries looking even more severe under the summer sun. Mark tried to call on his natural magic to heal him, but it just sparked and faded liked crossed wires.

"Thank you." Robert said, his black eyes fixed on Mark with an unusual intensity.

Not-Robert, Mark reminded himself. "You told me your name." Mark hoped by saying it out loud, it would help it make sense.

"It seemed like the right thing to do. I trust you." Robert winced as he tried to sit upright. "Which is positively insane, but it's the truth."

Mark wanted to reply that he didn't trust Robert, but the weight of the name hovered between them. All control had been given to Mark.

Robert saw the silent battle Mark was going through. "Name or not, I hope you can start to have some faith in me. Or at least believe that I was telling the truth when I said I'd never hurt you."

Sitting closely together in the grass, Robert's black eyes fixed on him with an unsettling intensity. Mark felt like an ignorant lump, compared to the depth of emotion that shone in Robert's gaze.

Mark felt a stab of fear, that this may go down a path he didn't want to travel. "Thank you, for doing what you could to protect Damian from that place."

At the mention of his host, the moment was broken. A flicker of disappointment crossed Robert's face. "I'll try and keep him unconscious until we've had time to heal."

"If I take you back to his house, do you promise not to hurt his aunt?" Mark asked with a frown. The only alternative was taking him back to Mark's house. Mark didn't think Nanna nor Michelle would welcome that.

Robert gave him a disgusted look. "I have been living in that cottage for months, and never harmed a hair on that woman's head."

"Apart from the fire before Christmas…"

Robert looked like he'd forgotten that. "It was nothing, I was just being impatient."

"Well, no more bouts of impatience." Mark got to his feet, then helped Robert up beside him. "Let's get you back to Miss Cole's house."

They made slow progress the last half mile, with no magical horses or kelpies to carry them. The light was starting to fail on this long summer's day when they final reached the cottage. A few fire-damaged items were on the lawn, but otherwise, everything looked normal.

Mark rapped on the door.

Damian's Aunt Maggie answered in her dressing gown. Maggie rushed forward to hug her nephew, then paused when she saw the state he was in.

"What?"

"Miss Cole, meet Robert."

Chapter Twenty

Mark had stayed with Aunt Maggie, waiting for one of the other witches to arrive, so they could heal Robert, and keep an eye on him.

Damian's aunt was full of questions, but Mark had managed to postpone most of them, by insisting that Robert needed rest and to heal. He pointed out that they all had Damian's best interests at heart.

Half an hour later, Miriam arrived, still looking a mess from her night of drinking with Nanna.

"Maggs, please, I can explain-"

Maggie cut her off, and formally directed her towards the patient in the sitting room.

Mark saw this as his cue to leave. He borrowed Damian's new bike, guessing his boyfriend wouldn't be using it for a few days at least.

It was fully dark by the time Mark got home, but he knew the way off by heart. Biking down the unlit country roads was oddly peaceful after everything that had happened.

Soon enough, his house came into view, and Mark rode up the driveway. He headed for his parents' side of the house, when he spotted Nanna standing at her door, arms crossed.

Sighing deeply, Mark turned obediently towards his Nanna, ready for whatever punishment was going to happen.

The old woman turned and led into the kitchen, starting to make tea in silence. Mark watched her carefully, his Nanna still looked tired, but it was heartening to see she was no longer the wreck she had been this morning.

After what seemed like an eternity, the kettle whistled, and Nanna served them both big mugs of tea. She sat near him on the table, assessing him closely.

"Nanna, I had no choice-" Mark started, but stopped when she raised a hand.

"I know, Michelle explained." She said quietly.

"Soo... I'm not getting told off?" Mark asked, hoping beyond hope.

"Oh, I wouldn't go that far. Just wait until your parents see you. Your Dad is fuming." Nanna gave a bitter smile.

Mark's heart sank. His relationship with his Dad had been stuttering since he accidentally used dark magic back in February. His Dad had explained how he had lost someone he cared about to dark magic. Now… Mark had thrown himself in the deep-end. On purpose.

"You are becoming your own man, Mark. Growing up is filled with having to make choices. The adults around you don't *always* know best." Nanna took his hand gently. "But know that we all want the best for you."

Mark sat quietly, warmed by the sentiment.

"Now, let's hear about your adventure."

Mark spent the next hour discussing everything that had happened, from the fire at Damian's, to the flying horse in the demon realm. Nanna had kept their mugs of tea filled, and listened with a sense of bemusement.

"D'you think there will be any trouble from the break-out?" Mark asked.

"They're all in a different realm – that might be enough to dissuade them from retaliating." Nanna replied. "Whatever happens, we'll all work together."

Mark chewed his lip, he hadn't *verbally* agreed to anything with the Governor; but the memory of her possessive gaze made him shudder.

"How are you feeling?" Nanna eyed him carefully. "That was a lot of dark magic you funnelled. And heaven knows what that weird blonde demon did to you."

"I felt like I'd been thrown into a wall, when I left the demon realm behind." Mark shrugged. "I think I'm OK now... just a little wired..."

"Well, be prepared for it to get worse." Nanna warned. "At least you can speak to Michelle about it, she's sure to be helpful and sympathetic... in her own way."

Mark frowned, thinking of how long it had taken to get Michelle clean from dark magic – or clean enough to get on with her life. He'd used more magic, but over a shorter period of time. How long would it affect Mark? Days, weeks, months?

He had his exams to finish, and Prom was only a week away. As much as Mark was willing to pay any price to keep Damian safe, he still hoped they could go to Prom together.

Then there was another event on the horizon. The Summer Solstice was fast approaching. When Mark would step up as Grand High Witch.

He picked nervously at a wooden knot on the table. "Have I ruined... will everything still go to plan at solstice?" Mark asked, not sure which answer would give him more comfort.

"I'm sure you'll be fine by then." Nanna said, patting his hand. "Worst case scenario – we delay it a few months, it's not the end of the world."

"Yeah." Mark gave a brittle smile. "It's not like you've got anyone else lined up for the gig."

Nanna gave a funny tilt of her head, but didn't say anything to confirm or deny it.

"Nanna, there aren't any other heirs, are there?" Mark asked carefully.

"Well, there's your cousin."

"Nanna, I don't have a cousin. Mum and Dad are both only children."

"That's not entirely true." Nanna replied, her tone of nonchalance not hitting quite right.

"Which part exactly, isn't true?"

"Technically, your Dad has an older sister. Her daughter is about the same age as you." Nanna said, her eyes drifting up.

Mark had no idea what she was talking about. If his Dad had a sister, he would have told him. He would have loved to have a bigger family. If he had a cousin, they would probably learn magic together, and he'd have someone who understood the pressure of being a potentially powerful witch...

His gaze drifted upward, following Nanna's.

"MICHELLE?"

"Keep your voice down, poor girl didn't sleep last night." Nanna hushed him.

"And whose fault was that?" Mark replied on auto-pilot, the rest of his thoughts not having caught up. "Michelle? But that means Edith...?"

"Is my daughter." Nanna confirmed.

"But she hates you!"

"Unfortunately, there is no law against that."

"How didn't I know about this?" Mark frowned. He'd always thought that Tealford was a happy place without secrets. The town had always been very open about the witches living there. Had they all been conspiring to withhold the truth?

"No one knows, just me and your Dad." Nanna said.

She got to her feet and re-filled the teapot, making sure they had a steady supply of tea.

Mark watched his Nanna warily. His whole life, he had worshipped the ground she walked on. Now he found out she'd lied about her health, and even about having a daughter.

"Edith, is five years older than your father, but the two of them were thick as thieves growing up. Michael used to follow her around constantly, and she absolutely adored him. I trained them both in witchcraft. Edith was a natural at it; your Dad was more interested in playing football."

Mark listened to the witchy version of an idyllic life. "What happened?"

"When Edith was fourteen, I was promoted to Grand High Witch." Nanna broke off and sighed. "Y'know, I wouldn't have won any parenting medals back then, but I thought we were doing alright up to that point. Then overnight, I went from mother of two, to matriarch of all the northern covens. Edith misread my obligation to duty, she always thought I was driven by ambition and a desire for power. It was kinda hard to deny her accusations, and I wonder if there was a little truth in them. Becoming the Grand High Witch was all-consuming, I don't think I could've given it up and gone back to regular magic. It was more than just the power; it was the responsibility that went with it. Witches turned to me for help every day, and it was like I found my calling in life, to be that *needed*."

Nanna broke off to sip at her tea, and Mark imagined she was gathering her strength for what came next.

"Edith and I did a lot of falling out. I don't think we agreed on anything over the next couple of years. The harder she made life at home, the more I threw myself into my role. It was wrong of me to try and escape, and I wonder every day, what might have happened if I'd spent more time with her.

"Feeling that power was the only thing that bought my attention, Edith started going out, dabbling in dark magic. She'd come home reeking of it, but when I tried to reason with her… we were so used to disagreeing, it just pushed her more to the dark stuff. She was becoming a dangerously powerful and unstable witch. Not a good combo."

Nanna sighed, and there was a flash of orange fur as Tigger the cat jumped into her lap, sensing that his therapy was needed. Nanna smiled as he started to purr, running her fingers through his ginger coat before she continued.

"When she was seventeen, Edith disappeared for a week. She was on the trail of some demon, and when she came home she was buzzing with dark magic. We got into another argument, and it was the first time she used magic against me. I can still remember the amount of *hate* that was behind that spell. Her emotions fuelled it, and she lost control.

"Michael was twelve then, and he'd always been the mediator when it was just words being flung. He foolishly tried to get between us, and Edith's dark magic hit him, almost killing him. Edith fled, and I didn't hear from her for a long time, until she popped back up on the radar when she started a coven of dark witches in London."

Mark sat, processing the story. It was hard to relate the girl in pain that Nanna described, with the evil woman who wanted to torture and kill him. And his poor Dad… no wonder he was nervous about Mark learning magic.

"How come I never heard about this? The coven didn't say anything when we went to London to face Edith."

"I warned you before, that even skilled witches can lose control." Nanna explained, with a shrug. "I was so distraught and betrayed by what Edith had done, and I had the most powerful magic at my command. It raised up in response to my desires, and rippled out across the County, removing Edith from living memory. In the end, only me, your Dad and Grandad remembered. I suppose it couldn't rewrite the deep connections… but we rarely spoke of her again."

"Does Michelle know?"

Nanna shook her head. "No, that poor girl has had enough to deal with recently, I didn't want to add to her troubles."

"She needs to know." Mark insisted. He thought of Michelle's hunt for her real family, which had led her to Edith in London. Now she had even more.

"I'll tell her soon." Nanna said unconvincingly.

Chapter Twenty-One

The night of Prom, Mark pulled on his tux and spruced himself up, as many Tealford teenagers were doing the same.

He'd managed to get one of the last suits from the York Outlet centre. It wasn't perfect, but it was better than borrowing his Dad's old suit. The collar on the shirt was a bit tight, Mark ended up leaving it unfastened. He felt like a fool, a kid playing dress up; but at least, with Damian as his date, no one would give Mark a second look. He'd happily hide in his fashionable boyfriend's shadow.

Mark's hands shook a little. The withdrawal from dark magic made it feel like his nerves were on fire. He'd tried to hide it as much as possible from his friends and family, knowing that he'd put them through enough stress already.

He picked up the small piece of jet Michelle had given him, and concentrated on slowing his breathing. Mark could sense the crystal drawing out the lingering darkness, and calming his nerves.

"Mark, stop preening, you're gonna be late." His Mum shouted up the stairs.

Mark sighed, pocketing the piece of jet, He checked his reflection one last time, before joining his family downstairs. His Mum insisted on photos, first Mark standing on his own, and then with his Dad.

Mark was more than bored, when Michelle and Nanna let themselves in.

Michelle was wearing a navy dress that suited her pale skin. Her usually-frizzy dark brown hair was pinned up in shiny loose curls.

"Wow, you look nice." Mark said, surprised at how different she looked.

Michelle gave an unladylike shrug. "Your Mum took me dress shopping, and Nanna did my hair. I think they like having a girl around to do girly stuff."

More photos followed, until Mark worried he would get permanent flashes behind his eyes.

Eventually, his Dad broke them up, and steered them to the car. They headed to the local golf club, picking up Damian on the way.

The golf club was set on a vast country estate, and the grand manor house sat intimidatingly at the end of a long gravel driveway.

As they got out of the car, Mark was aware of Michelle's gooseberry status. "You're welcome to stay with us."

"Nah, I've got a date."

"Who? Not that dark witch dude from Sheffield?" Mark grimaced at the thought of the sleazy guy who had mooned over Michelle.

"Ha, he wishes!" Michelle snorted.

Michelle looked across the crowd, and spied her date. One of the quiet guys from her group of outsiders. He looked stunned by her appearance. Michelle smirked, appreciating the reaction.

She glanced back at Mark and Damian. "Still not your friend."

Mark watched as she strode away from them. No, not friend. Cousin.

"You alright?" Damian asked, nudging him out of his thoughts.

"Yeah." Mark replied, looking at his boyfriend. "I should be asking you that. You sure you're healed enough for this?"

"I wouldn't miss this for the world." Damian gave a weak smile, then winced at the fading bruise on his cheek. "Although we may have to forgo any wrestling in the gardens."

"Pity." Mark held out his hand. "Let's do Prom."

Damian took the offered hand, his fingers curling gently around Mark's. "Let's."

They made their way inside, receiving less-than-subtle looks at Damian's array of bruises. Mark wondered what the other pupils would come up with this time. Then he decided that he didn't care. School was over, and they had a long and glorious summer ahead of them. A few weak rumours were nothing compared to what Mark had been through.

Mark led to the table that they were sharing with Harry, Sarah, and a couple of Damian's fellow footballers.

"You scrubbed up well." Mark elbowed Harry.

"Thanks, Sarah coordinated us." His best friend replied, proudly.

Mark snorted, but didn't have chance to say anything else. Waiters brought food to their tables, and the entire Prom went quiet, focussing on the fantastic meal.

Once the meal was finished, they were persuaded to step outside, whilst the tables were pushed back and a dance floor created.

Mark filed out with the others, his hand intertwined with Damian's. There was a bubbling energy from the students, they seemed to be celebrating and commiserating the fact that they had finally finished school. They were free, and a little bit terrified about it.

Mark spotted Dean hovering by the door with some girls. They had both avoided each other since Dean's drunken confessions; and Mark didn't want to break their clean run. He veered aside, and led Damian to a quieter part of the dimly-lit grounds.

"You remember what I said about no physically exertive trysts in the gardens?" Damian asked.

"Don't you trust me?" Mark teased.

"With my life." Damian said, in quiet seriousness.

His tone made Mark halt in his stride. "Damian…"

"You're my hero. You're my everything." Damian pulled him closer, his hands running up the thin white shirt that covered Mark's arms.

Mark leant closer to kiss him, but jumped as cold water splashed against his face. A few lonely heavy drops hit the ground around them, followed by a million more.

The rain quickly soaked them through, but Damian simply laughed, tilting his head up. "Give me a break - I thought this was supposed to be summer!"

"A Yorkshire summer." Mark reminded him, smiling at his boyfriend's reaction. "Let's go in."

"No, I want you to myself for a minute more." Damian replied, his hands tightening on Mark's arms.

The rain was suddenly a background nuisance, and all that mattered was his boyfriend. Mark's heart ached for him. "I know you might not be in the same place as me, but…"

"I love you." Damian whispered in his ear, kissing his jaw. "I always have."

"Really? I mean… I thought when you didn't say it back, that I was jumping the gun." Mark rattled on nervously.

Damian moved to look him square in the eye, rain trickling down his sharp cheekbones. "Yes, but that was immediately after Eadric was killed – a part of me was worried that it was a reaction to losing him. Then I panicked and thought that, if I said I loved you that night, maybe you'd think it was a pity response, or because it's the socially-expected reply."

"I think we've both been over-thinking it." Mark said with an embarrassed smile. "I love you."

"And I've loved you since the day you rescued me from the snow last winter. For six months I've been terrified of saying anything, because I don't deserve you. I don't think I ever will." Damian bit his lip. "But recent events have made me appreciate life more. I'm going to spend every day from now on, proving that I love you."

Mark leant forward, slowly closing the distance and capturing his boyfriend's lips beneath his. Under the dark, raining sky, they would have a perfect moment of happiness.

Other books by K.S. Marsden:

Witch-Hunter ~ *Now available in audiobook*
The Shadow Rises (Witch-Hunter #1)
The Shadow Reigns (Witch-Hunter #2)
The Shadow Falls (Witch-Hunter #3)

Witch-Hunter trilogy box-set

Witch-Hunter Prequels
James: Witch-Hunter (#0.5)
Sophie: Witch-Hunter (#0.5)
Kristen: Witch-Hunter (#2.5) ~ coming 2021

Enchena
The Lost Soul: Book 1 of Enchena
The Oracle: Book 2 of Enchena

Northern Witch
Winter Trials (Northern Witch #1)
Awaken (Northern Witch #2)
The Breaking (Northern Witch #3)
Summer Sin (Northern Witch #4)

Printed in Great Britain
by Amazon

69671850R00129